Stolen

Stolen

ARABELLA KINGSLEY

Thought Catalog Books

Brooklyn, NY

THOUGHT CATALOG BOOKS

Copyright © 2016 by Arabella Kingsley

All rights reserved. Published by Thought Catalog Books, a division of The Thought & Expression Co., Williamsburg, Brooklyn. Founded in 2010, Thought Catalog is a website and imprint dedicated to your ideas and stories. We publish fiction and non-fiction from emerging and established writers across all genres. For general information and submissions: manuscripts@thoughtcatalog.com.

First edition, 2016

ISBN 978-1945796302

10 9 8 7 6 5 4 3 2 1

Cover photography by © g-stockstudio

Contents

Prologue

He stole her from him by force. Stole back what was rightfully his. Now he was her king. She was his to own, to dominate and rule, to love without condition, to cherish and to worship. He would bind her to him for an eternity and never let her go. There would be no escape.

But life has a way of twisting fate, intention, and purpose. There would be challenges to his claim upon her by three. One would seek to take her from him for himself, a second would try to destroy her, and a third to confine her in his power and cage her before the game was truly won and the prize was claimed.

1

Handsome American billionaire Mark Dexter looked down at the pretty woman draped frontways over his desk, her hands tied behind her back with his fine silk purple tie and her skirt around her waist. He continued pulling her black silk panties down to her ankles and over her feet kicking in high heels which, to his amusement, didn't reach the floor.

"You can't do this. You can't just spank me like a child. Let me go now or I will scream the place down," the woman shouted in her upper-crust English accent, doing her best to wrestle her small, curvy body off the desk onto the floor.

He pulled the panties away from her and rested his hand on the middle of her back in an effort to calm and steady her.

"I have every right to discipline you. I caught you stealing documents from my office. I am ruler of my domain, Ms. Sumner," he said with some amusement in his tone. "And I don't tolerate spies and thieves."

Mark cast his black eyes over her pert pale bottom lifting off the table toward him. It reminded him of a juicy ripe peach he wanted to take a bite out of.

"I had no choice. He sent me. He made me." There was a plea in her voice.

"I can imagine. But you could have come to me. You know that. I am going to send your husband a message. He is messing with the wrong man. I won't let him ruin my business and steal it for himself."

Mark nodded at the second man in the room, who was a member of his security team. He held up a smartphone to continue filming the scene with a grin, homing in on the billionaire James Sumner's wife's bare bottom being prepared for a firm spanking.

Mark smoothed the back of his hand against one ripe buttock, loving the feel of her skin against his hand. He'd wanted to see the woman naked and beneath him in his bed for a long time. She was married to a brute of a man he'd been forced to do business with, and Mark Dexter had dreamed of a way to get her away from him and into the security of his own arms. He hadn't expected her to betray him like this. He still held her panties in the other hand, and as she continued to bleat, an idea struck him hard. Pulling her body up off the desk by her tied hands, he scrunched the silky material up and pushed the garment in between her lips to gag her.

Grinning at her mumbles against the makeshift gag, Mark exchanged a satisfied look with the man filming the proceedings. He placed his hand in the middle of her back once more, and standing to the side he raised his hand to deliver the first slap. Drew Sumner's body tightened and jerked, lifting into the air with the first hard strike. Her bare bottom wobbled and shook with the force. The billionaire hit the opposite buttock, delighted when the reaction was reproduced. He then spanked the seat of her rump.

Drew whimpered, cried, and squirmed as he increased the pace of his strikes, diverting his attention momentarily to the tender backs of her thighs.

"This will teach you not to be a naughty little girl and sneak in people's offices to steal information," he mocked in a fatherly tone. He looked into the camera, another idea forming in his head. "Maybe next time you can come and confront me yourself instead of putting your wife at risk," he told James Sumner in between the thwack of his hand against Drew's buttocks. "It's time someone taught you a lesson. If you want your wife back, return the documents and contact book you made Drew steal the last time she was here, or this video goes all over YouTube, Twitter, Facebook, and other media. Until then your wife is mine. Consider her stolen."

Drew lay over the table crying, prompting Mark to rest his hand on top of her sore, burning bottom. He looked at his aide holding the phone.

"Send James Sumner the video," he ordered, removing the gag from Drew's mouth.

The man nodded and sent the video. Mark gestured for the man to leave the phone on the desk and make his exit from the room. Alone, Mark gently smoothed his palm over one of Drew's hot cheeks to soothe it. He leaned forward and pulled the panties carefully from her mouth and deposited them in the bin at the side. She wouldn't be needing them again. He sighed and continued to rub her butt cheek, listening to her cry.

"There, there. It's all over. Now tell me why you betrayed me, Drew. I thought you and I were good friends." He listened to the frustration and annoyance in his voice and tried to dampen it. He knew fine well why she'd done it. He could see the bruising on her cheek from here. What had James threatened her with now? Mark suddenly felt protective of the woman. "This isn't the first time you've stolen from me. I wondered if it was you the last time things went missing from my office. I refused to believe it was you. Now I know. Come on, talk to me."

The American billionaire gave her buttock one sharp spank, flaring the heat once more when she declined to answer.

"Answer me now," he commanded, raising his hand again to deliver another lash.

"He hit me. But that isn't the worst of it. I can take that. I am used to it," she shouted. "He has taken Eva from me."

Mark poised his hand in mid-air.

"Your daughter?"

"Yes. She's only three and I don't know where she is. He stole her away from the house I am renting. I left him. I thought I was secure this time, but he always finds me. Two of his men took her away in a car while he dragged me back home. He told me that if I didn't do as I was told I would never see her again. He threatened to kill her, Mark. How could he do that to his own daughter? I am sorry," she sobbed, "but I did what I had to. Now I fear he will kill her."

Frowning, Mark lowered his hand and cupped both of her butt cheeks. He moved his hands up and down to massage her bare bottom to calm her agitation, trying to keep his own in check for the fear she must be feeling. It was time he took both Drew and her crippling situation in hand. She was a strong, determined woman who had tried to dig her own way out, but James Sumner was a ruthless opponent who would stop at nothing to get his own way. Mark Dexter knew that all too well from personal experience. Drew needed someone on her side. She needed someone fighting in her corner, someone with money and connections. Someone who loved her.

"Shhh. Relax," he whispered, bending to touch her bottom with his lips. Mark felt the heat scorching from it with approval. He stood by his decision to spank her. She had stolen from him and had warranted the punishment for committing the act of theft, and more importantly, for not coming to him for help.

"You should have come to me when you left him. I would have protected you and your child. I know James is abusive to you. I won't let him do anything to her or you again. We will get her back," he informed her in an even velvet tone to reassure her.

"No. You have to let me go back. I can't risk it. I think he has taken her out of the country, possibly back to England. We have a home in London and in Hertfordshire. It's a large estate. He has probably hidden her there. I have to find her. I am going out of my head."

Mark glanced down between his captive's thighs visible through her slightly parted legs as she lay face down on top of his desk, her arms still bound behind her back with his tie. Despite her distress, she was wet from her spanking. Tiny beads of moisture coated her soft pale insides. He slipped his fingers in between her legs, careful not to penetrate the pouting lips of her vagina, and stroked rhythmically, allowing the dampness to coat the pads of his fingers.

"No. You aren't going anywhere," he said, huskily tracing the curve of her vulva once more, careful not to enter. You will remain with me under my protection and under this roof where I can see you," he soothed. "I am in charge of the situation now and I will find your baby. I promise."

He heard Drew give a small gasp. She did not verbally protest at the intimacy of his touch, but the wriggle of her body on top of the desk told him she was torn as to whether or not to enjoy and be calmed by his caress.

"You have to let me go," she said breathlessly. "I have to go back to save Eva."

"Hush. I have waited a long time for the opportunity to steal you away from that monster." Mark's voice was dark and filled with anger, but it was controlled. "I am not letting go of you.

You will never be hit or attacked by James Sumner again. I will find your child and you will both live with me where I can keep you safe and loved."

"No. You don't have to do that. And besides I need my independence and…"

"Shhh." Mark raised his fingers a little higher until they hovered just over the periphery of her pussy and pressed down, moving his fingers back and forth.

Another helpless cry escaped her lips and silenced her dissent.

"I don't see you as an independent woman, Drew. You need a man to rule and school you—not with violence, but love. We both know that's right. That's why you are so wet now after being spanked. I know you and I also know you are in love with me as much as I am to you and always have been since we first met. I have just been waiting for the right opportunity to steal you back. That time has come, darling. Now I am taking back what is rightfully mine and no one is going to stop me," he told her confidently, arrogantly.

She answered him with a satisfied moan of pleasure.

"I have always belonged to you, Mark, and I always will. I can't deny the truth," she told him with intense feeling. "But I have to go back for Eva. What will you do if I try to leave?" she tested.

Mark gave a soft chuckle and picked up his caress, moving his finger just underneath one juicy plump lip. Her vagina was flooded.

The billionaire pulled Drew's blouse out of her skirt. He yanked it up her back and with one hand expertly undid the catch on her bra. It fell open, freeing the swell of flesh pressed into the desk. Wasting no time, he placed his hand underneath her body up under the open bra and cupped a large milky breast in his palm as she waited for his answer. He gave it a sharp squeeze, making her cry out in shock at the strength he exerted in his possessive hold.

"You won't be able to. My security is tight. It will be impossible."

"But if I escaped? If I managed to find a way? What would you do?" There was apprehension and curiosity in her tone.

Her hips and pelvis jerked when he circled the entrance to her channel and with a smile of satisfaction impaled her on his middle finger in one sharp, stabbing movement.

"You won't. I will never hurt you, Drew. I love you."

Her captor pulsed his finger in and out of her, knowing she was highly aroused and ready to cum. She began to pant and move down onto his digit.

"But if I catch you trying to, I will throw you over my knee, whip your bare ass with my belt, strip you naked, and chain you to your bed until you understand just who is in charge here," he told her, firmly giving her nipple a tight, hot pinch with his fingers.

Her gasp echoed around the room. Mark cruelly thrust his finger hard inside her body, making her buck like a wildcat, allowing him to enjoy the feel of the slippery wet muscles inside her channel attempting to grip him as he curled it upward to stroke her G-spot. Drew was unable to catch her breath, and Mark knew he had her exactly where he wanted.

"I meant what I said. I have stolen you from your husband and now you are mine. Now submit to me and cum."

Mark drew his hand away from her breast and slapped one butt cheek hard and continued to strike her bottom. It wasn't long before he was treated to a loud frantic moan through her cries, signaling her climax. Spurred by the eruption of her passion, he continued to strike her bottom until she was spent and her body slumped onto the desk exhausted.

2

Mark had no choice but to leave Drew to assign his security team the task of locating the whereabouts of Eva and attend a business meeting. He couldn't believe his luck. Drew was firmly in his arms and in his power. He'd waited so long to take her from his rival and she had simply fallen helplessly into his lap. He straightened his tie and smoothed his hand around the groomed facial hair adorning his jawline and around his mouth as he walked toward the lounge to meet the billionaire Madeleine Cross. They were partners in a joint construction project for a new shopping mall, an exclusive apartment block, and a hotel, but her building-supplies company hadn't been delivering on time. As a result, the project was being delayed and in danger of not being delivered on time, making him incur substantial loss. Time to teach her a lesson for her tardiness before attending to his beautiful Drew. He brushed his hand over his clothed cock as he walked down the corridor, feeling it still hard and taut in his suit trousers eager to be inside her. He grinned, knowing he would not be able to hide it from Madeleine.

Confident and arrogant, he walked into the lounge where she sat sipping coffee from a white china cup and saucer rimmed with gold. He'd kept her waiting and her red lips were pouting with annoyance when he entered the room in his New York apartment. She was seductive in her scarlet close-fitting dress with her black hair tied back painfully tight in a ponytail from her face. She was attractive but not his type. Still, he would have liked a bite of the cherry just to taste and sample.

"Madeleine. It's good to see you," he said, softly bending over her to give her a quick kiss on the cheek.

"Mark. I don't take kindly to being summoned. What am I doing here?" she said abruptly.

He made sure he sat down next to her, watching her eyes sweep lustily over him.

"You know why, Madeleine? You have been holding back on the supplies and doing a deal behind my back with James Sumner to sabotage the project and ruin me. What has he promised you? To help you out of the debt you are incurring from the Logan project that failed?"

"You are crazy. I have done no such thing."

She leaned forward to put her cup and saucer down on the glass table in front of her and made to get up from the sofa, no doubt to storm out.

"I don't have to take this."

As she stood, Mark reached up and caught hold of her arm. He brought her back down onto the sofa hard.

"We both know I am telling the truth," he told her in a dark, seductive voice, tracing his thumb from the middle of her delicate wrist up her arm and back. She studied him closely.

"No. No I didn't. I can explain. There has just been a delay on…"

Mark allowed his thumb to travel back up her arm, and this time when it reached the middle he raised it and gently pushed it between her pouting red lips to silence her. He pressed down on her tongue, making her chocolate brown eyes stare at him.

"Hush," he said smoothly, beginning to slowly pulse his thumb in and out of her mouth, delighting in the smooth, wet feel. "Enough lying," he whispered, leaning close. His free hand slid up inside her tight dress up onto the soft flesh of her pale thigh above the top of her nude stocking and stroked the pads of his manicured fingers toward the aperture between her thighs.

"I don't like to be lied to. I am a good judge of character and I have to confess I was never sure of yours."

Mark pulled his thumb out of her juicy mouth and rhythmically circled it around her red satin lips. He heard her pant and watched her breasts heave with arousal. The billionaire trailed his finger underneath her panties and sank them into the folds of her vagina. Her pelvis bucked in response. He looked upon her with a satisfied smile. She was already becoming wet. He pushed his thumb back into her mouth and slowly moved it in and out between her lips. Her eyes glazed and her ruby-tipped fingernails dug into the cream leather sofa as he pinched and kneaded her clit.

He paused for a moment to drag her red satin panties down her legs to the floor, removing his thumb in her mouth to roughly take her lips and kiss her deeply, dominantly. She whimpered with the force of his male strength but still did not remove her hands from the sofa to hold onto him. Cold to the last, he thought idly with amusement. He smiled, satisfied against her lips when he heard her move and step out of her panties in her Louboutins.

Pulling back, he replaced his thumb and then inserted his middle finger up inside her pussy with one sharp thrust. She bucked and began to suck like a baby on his thumb, enjoying the way he pushed it down on her tongue and thrusted it in and out in time with his finger inside her vagina. On the third push of his finger inside her channel, he increased the pace of his rhythm until he could feel her close.

"I don't like to be fucked with," he sternly informed her.

Unable to help herself, the naughty Miss Cross was moving her pelvis frantically against his fingers and pushing down on them, undeterred by his words. Her eyes were closed as she sucked on his thumb and moaned with need. With a cruel smile, he added a third finger inside her, making her cry out with surprise. His thumb worked her clit by flexing it back and forth as he curled his three digits up to the rough back wall of her pussy deep inside and smoothed their tips over it.

"You see if I catch anyone fucking with me I always fuck them back and harder. They learn never to go against me again. It's a hard lesson to learn, Miss Cross, but one that you have to."

Her eyes flew open but his internal caress became frantic and before she could push him away, she was cumming hard. Like a woman possessed she cried and moaned around his thumb as it fucked her mouth and his fingers took her pussy without remorse.

Finally she fell back against the sofa, defeated. Mark's thumb remained in her mouth still moving in and out as she recovered her breath. His aide Michael appeared as if on cue. He leaned over the sofa and grinned at his employer, watching him slow the pace of his fingers moving in and out of Miss Cross's vagina clearly displayed after the skirt of her dress had risen up when she had agitatedly squirmed and moved on the sofa.

"Sir, your guest is now upstairs being prepared for you as you requested."

"Thank you, Michael. I will go to her as soon as I am finished with Miss Cross here."

Michael grinned and nodded before leaving the room. A cloud darkened over Miss Cross's face. Mark removed his thumb and put his finger immediately to her lips.

"Hush. I will not hear any more from you."

Removing his fingers from her pussy, he inserted them into his mouth and licked the cream from them.

"Yum. Such a lovely taste. It is a shame we won't be able to play anymore. But I don't deal with liars."

He leaned down and picked her panties off the floor. Standing, he tossed them onto her lap while she still panted.

"Take them with you when you leave. Consider our agreement at an end. I will carry the project myself. And if I ever catch you trying to sabotage my business again with or without the help of James Sumner I will ruin you, Miss Cross. Now leave before I have you thrown out."

He fastened the button on his suit jacket and left the room, not bothering to give her a second glance. Time to attend to little Drew and assert his authority over her in a primal, primitive way.

Mark strode along the corridor to the room he'd had Drew placed in, glancing out of the large glass windows looking out over Manhattan and the other tall buildings covering the landscape. He would never get used to the splendor of the view. It took his breath away every time he looked at it.

He was surprised to find his heart racing with excitement when he took hold of the round gold handle to open the door. For a moment he stopped and listened to Drew's helpless pants of desire and cries of outrage as his assistant pleasured her in a way he had no doubt she had never experienced before. He grinned to himself when he heard the slap of pert bare flesh echo loudly. And again. His little Drew's bottom would be very sore tonight and would no doubt need the loving caress of his massaging hand and moisturizer to soothe the burn from her spankings. Mark listened some more, enjoying the anticipation of what he would eventually find when he opened the door.

"You will remain still, little girl, or I will clamp your clit and whip your breasts until you learn to behave. Mr. Dexter likes an obedient woman beneath him when he mounts her, not a churlish, insubordinate one. You may have had free rein with your husband, but here Mr. Dexter rules all of his women and his house with an iron rod." Gill, his pretty young assistant, was schooling Drew to his approval. She spoke the truth and as soon as Drew understood his dominance over her, the better their relationship would be or she would spend most of her time over his knee being disciplined with a bare-bottom spanking until she did.

"You make it sound like he has a harem." Drew's voice was breathless, tearful. "How can he do this to me?"

He heard the bed move and squeak. Gill grunted hard and Drew gave a loud cry. The noise grew louder and more frantic. Mark felt his hardness painfully increase, knowing exactly what Gill was doing to Drew. He covered it with his hand to soothe it, yet he waited a while longer before entering.

"He does of sorts." Gill was panting now. "You will be ruled just like the rest of us in his employment and you will come to love and respect it as we all do. Now remain still and allow me to thrust harder. I want to be deeper inside you. All the way to the hilt. Mr. Dexter wants you stretched and prepared for mounting. You have a lovely feel. Such a wet, pretty pussy; I am going to enjoy tasting it later."

Mark closed his eyes, feeling desire burn inside the pit of his stomach and need shake his body. Wasting no more time, he opened the door and walked into the room.

His breath caught in his throat. Drew was completely naked, face-down with her shoulders resting on top of the bed, her wrists tied behind her back. Gill knelt behind her with a dildo strapped to her waist. It was embedded deep inside Drew's vagina and his assistant was pumping it hard and fast out of Drew with the powerful thrust of her hips. One hand was beneath Drew stroking her pussy, harshly pinching at her delicate clit while the other leaned forward and tugged on her head, forcing it up and back uncomfortably. For all her protest, Drew's body was actively betraying it by pushing back onto the dildo.

Mark watched, enjoying the sight of Gill's dominance over Drew and the way her breasts bounced on her chest almost in unison with the jump of Drew's plump globes as she was pounded. It was a mouth-watering sight to behold.

"Mark. Stop this," Drew bleated, but he could detect the tell-tale signs of want singing in her tone.

She was just too ashamed to admit it. In time, she would learn to feel no fear in pushing her sexual boundaries with him for both his pleasure and hers. Had she been distressed he would have put a stop to the whole scene straightaway, but he was more than satisfied she was enjoying the new experience and she was being cared for.

"Sir. I didn't see you," Gill said, slowing her pace. "Do you wish me to dismount her?"

Mark sat in one of two armchairs and shook his head.

"No, please continue," he instructed, making himself comfortable. He turned to the second chair at the young man sitting there relaxed, watching the two women with great interest. Tomas was the billionaire's male assistant who was there to take care of running his business with Gill when he couldn't be there. Mark liked balance in his work life and would never entrust the responsibility of running his business to just one person. But Tomas had an extra task that Gill didn't have. Mark Dexter was very protective of his female staff. If he was away and they required protection, assistance, or discipline, Tomas would be there to bestow it on his behalf.

He was present to make sure Drew was cared for and her needs met as Gill prepared her in a robust manner for taking.

"She is very beautiful, Sir," Tomas said. "And she moistens quick. You have been waiting a long time to have her in your bed again. You must be ecstatic," he smiled.

Mark grinned.

"Yes, I am." He paused and issued Gill with an order.

"Make her cum. Tomas, mount Gill so she feels the pleasure of a climax as well."

"Mark, no. This is so humiliating…"

Drew's voice trailed off, a loud moan of need echoing out from her lips when Gill nipped her clit and kneaded it again, rolling it back and forth between her bright, pink-tipped nails.

Tomas grinned at him and stood, loosening his tie.

"And before you do, gag Drew with your tie."

Gill continued to ride Drew like there was no tomorrow and threw Tomas a longing glance as he undressed. Mark knew fine well they were together despite their efforts to keep it secret. They couldn't hide the way they looked at each other when together.

Tomas walked toward the bed unhindered by his nakedness. His long, thick, impressive cock was taut and ready for action. He took his purple tie over to Drew and holding it tightly forced it between her lips as she opened her mouth to take an agitated breath. Mark could see her eyes were glazed and she was now lost in pleasure despite her whimpers. However shocked she was that she was being ridden by a woman with a strap-on, she couldn't deny her arousal at being penetrated.

Tomas tied her gag securely at the back of her head and took up position behind Gill. Without warning he wound his hand inside her blonde curls and twisted his fingers, making a fist shape. He pulled her head back against his chest and slipped his fingers inside her pussy. She appeared heavily wet to Mark by the glistening beads of dampness coating the tops of her thighs. Tomas wasted no time in bending her slightly forward over Drew, making her go deeper inside the woman. Satisfied she was in position, he guided and thrusted his long cock up inside her vagina in one brutal motion. Gill groaned and sighed with contentment as Tomas forced her up, arching her back and head. Once comfortable with the pace of his thrust, she continued with Drew.

Tomas speared slow, hard, and deep. Gill's body jumped with the savage force Tomas used to fuck her, sending shock waves through Drew. Mark watched intently as the threesome moved in perfect harmony with Tomas at the lead governing the whole proceedings. Picking up the rhythm to thrust manically inside Gill, he struck one buttock with his hand three times. Mark let out a breath, reveling at the way her plump rump wobbled with the contact of his hand.

"Cum now, bitch," he ordered.

Gill thrusted faster inside Drew, reaching to cup and slap her pussy with her hand. Drew gave a loud cry as Gill screamed when Tomas slapped her bottom again

"Now, bitch, make sure the woman you are fucking cums with you or I will take my belt to your bottom."

Mark raised an amused eyebrow, noticing how Gill responded instantly to Tomas's firm direction and the title of bitch.

With another slap to her rear end, his assistant was screaming her climax as Drew's own muffled cries grew hot and frantic against the gag. A second later Tomas grunted and growled, driving into Gill in cruel fashion until they were all spent.

Mark couldn't help but give the ensemble a clap. The scene had been stimulating and intensified his desire for Drew. He couldn't wait any longer to be inside her. He stood loosening his tie and unbuttoning his shirt. Tomas kissed Gill and took hold of the end of the dildo to carefully slip it out of Drew. He and Gill left the bed. Taking hold of Gill's hand, he led her out of the room to leave Mark and Drew alone.

Drew was still breathing hard into her gag when the billionaire approached the bed in his unbuttoned shirt. He rested his hand on her back and rubbed it back and forth to calm her, delighting in the feel of the sheen of sweat lightly coating her soft, pale skin. Her long gold curls cascaded over her back. She was beautiful. Soft and vulnerable lying between the white silk sheets. She turned her head slightly, staring at him with her sea-blue eyes treating him to a glimpse of the faded bruising on her neck where her husband had tried to strangle her in a fit of rage. His frame tightened, thinking of the way she had been brutalized. He finished undressing. He wouldn't let anything happen to her ever again. Now that she was firmly in his care, he could protect her. He untied her hands and lay them carefully at her sides.

Mark loosened the gag from her mouth. He wanted to hear her cries of pleasure this time.

"Mark, why did you make me do that? I have never been with a woman before."

He smiled gently, unable to resist the urge to lean over and give her cheek a kiss.

"Did you enjoy it?" he asked in a seductive whisper, caressing his hand over the curve of one plump buttock.

There was a pause. His smile widened.

"It was a new experience for me," she said quietly, a slight trace of confused amusement in her voice.

"I will take that as a yes."

"I had rather it had been you inside me."

With one fluid motion Mark took hold of her hips and forced her to turn over onto her back. He caught hold of her hands and lifted her arms up above her head and held them there, holding her in place. She gasped with the quickness of the movement and lay looking up at him.

"I have waited a long time to have you underneath me again. This time it will be forever. I will never let you go again. Now open your legs and let me inside you so I can reclaim you. Once you are divorced from him I will marry you like I should have done five years ago and make you conceive our own child."

With one hard thrust he embedded his cock inside her pussy to the hilt to emphasize his resolve and started to ride her hard.

3

Mark continued to thrust as deeply as he could inside Drew, holding her hands above her head with one hand while his other closed around her throat in a gentle but firm chokehold. He pumped his cock slowly and deeply, tightening his hold around her throat, watching her eyes glaze with pleasure at the pure dominance he exercised over her.

He felt every muscle in his body ripple with the strength of his movement. His shoulder tensed, pulling taut the large black tattoo he'd gotten when in the New York gang The Lightning Brotherhood to show his allegiance. It was of a large lightning bolt with a sword in the middle and two fierce dragons curling around it. The image stretched down to just above his forearm and right around the top of his arm. There was no color in it, only black. Those days of belonging to the Brotherhood were now over, but he could never quite escape the connections to the gang which refused to sever. James Sumner was one. His second in command when Mark was finally given the honor of being made leader. James had always believed it should have been him.

Drew bucked back against him softly, moaning with delight at the way his slow movement caused his cock to stroke the velvet walls of her channel and tickle her G-spot. Now she was ready; it was time to get rough and unleash the dragon he'd kept hidden inside since she'd married James; it was time to remind her of whom she now belonged to.

The billionaire pulled out of her sharply and let go of her throat. He took hold of her and turned her over swiftly onto her front. Drew gave a surprised shriek as he pulled her arms behind her back and slipped his own through them. With a sharp tug, he forced her to rise from the bed toward the large reinforced glass windows. There were no curtains. His philosophy was to allow as much light as possible into the space, and curtains were a hindrance making him feel closed in. The New York landscape stretched out in front of him in the glorious hot sunshine. There wasn't a cloud around and the sky was a deep blue. The penthouse apartment was surrounded by other tall buildings, some exclusive offices, others apartments. He could see people milling about two floors below in one of the skyscrapers. Mark smiled to himself. They would be seen.

He wanted the world to see her naked and confined in his arms. She was his now and no one else would be allowed to take her from him. He slammed her frontways up against the window, making her breasts squash against the glass for a moment. Drew's small hands pushed against the glass to balance herself with a gentle whimper. She didn't protest at his rough handling; rather her skin appeared to flush a deep rosy pink with arousal and melted against him. They only complaint she made was,

"But we will be seen here," she panted. "Two men are watching us over there."

Mark glanced out and grinned. Satisfaction filled him. He wanted an audience for this.

The billionaire weaved his hand through gold red curls and pulled hard, forcing her head back. He looked down at her from the side.

"Good," he answered. "Now spread your legs and stick your butt out."

To encourage her he treated her to a firm slap across one already hot pink buttock. Her body jumped and her legs were opening quickly. She stuck out her bottom and thrusted her pussy back at him. Still maintaining his grip on her hair and clenching the tight muscles in his backside, he eased his tight cock back inside her and started to ram fast.

"Mark, oh Mark. I've waited so long to be with you. I never thought…" she cried, ready to cum.

He removed his hand from her waist and placed it over her mouth.

"Hush and cum. We are together again and no one will part us," he grunted, feeling himself close.

He moved harder but slightly slower, spearing her with sharp deep thrusts as though making a kill. Her scream of pleasure was muffled against his hand when her orgasm erupted. He came with her, his seed shooting like a torrent inside her. One day soon it would bear fruit in her womb.

Mark pulled the silk white sheet over Drew's sleeping form and kissed her shoulder before leaving her to take a shower. She looked a lot more relaxed. He allowed the hot steaming water to run over the taut muscle of his chest and closed his eyes, reveling that he had her back in his arms. Now it was time to plot revenge against James Sumner and put an end to his connection with Drew in marriage as soon as possible.

When he finished dressing in a dark grey suit with a red tie he called his lawyer in his office. He wanted divorce proceedings issued immediately. He was just finishing his call when the door to his office opened and Drew stood in the doorway wrapped in the sheet. His heart leapt; she looked sleepy, soft, and vulnerable. He felt his muscled body tense with the need to catch her up in his arms to protect her. He stood up and approached her as she closed the door behind her.

"I couldn't find my clothes," she gushed with a small blush lighting her cheeks.

He smoothed his hands over her bare shoulders and kissed her lips.

"You don't need them. I want you naked when we are alone. There is no need for you to wear clothes. I want to be able to touch you, caress you, and mount you when I want," he whispered huskily, tugging at the top of the sheet until it came loose.

With a quick snapping movement, he swept it away from her and let it fall in a silken pool on the floor next to her naked body. She gasped and tried to cover herself, but with a smile he pulled her arms away, sweeping his dark eyes over her form before drawing her into the confinement of his arms.

The quick movement appeared to make her head spin and she slumped in his arms ready to faint. Full of concern, he swept his hand around the side of her face to cup it and raise it up to him, supporting her falling body with his strong arm.

"Drew, what's wrong? Are you all right?"

Her eyes fluttered closed and then opened again.

"I just feel a bit faint."

"I will have my doctor called."

Mark slipped an arm underneath her legs and carried her to one of the leather chairs in front of his desk. He sat down with her on his lap and reached for the phone on his desk. She stopped him.

"No, please. It's nothing. I haven't been eating very well. James confined me to my bedroom and starved me until I capitulated. I was only allowed a little water."

Mark caressed the pads of his fingers along her cheek, feeling anger rise hot and fierce inside him. He wanted to kill James Sumner.

"How long did he do this for?"

"Two weeks."

"Shit, Drew, I need you checked out by a doctor."

He reached for the phone again and once more she stopped him.

"No. I will be all right. You know I hate doctors."

He shook his head and pulled his hand holding the phone out from under hers.

"No. I want you checked out. Don't argue with me, baby girl. Remember I am in charge now and I will take care of you."

Cradling her in his arms on his lap, he tapped the speed dial for his private doctor. Drew gave a sigh and relaxed, pressing her face against his chest and surrendering to his control. Satisfied, he trailed his fingers up and down her arm as he spoke to the man.

"Doctor Travers is unavailable but he is sending one of his team around just to give you a quick check over. He suspects it is exhaustion and some malnutrition. He wants you back in bed," Mark told her, putting his mobile down on the desk again and standing up with her in his arms.

Before he started carrying her back to the bedroom he looked down at her, unable to stop himself from asking, "Why the hell did you leave me and marry him? When we argued and you left that night after I proposed you said you weren't ready for marriage."

Drew stared up at him with sudden tears in her eyes, clearly acknowledging the pain in his voice.

"I didn't have a choice. My family forced me into marriage with James. Two days after I walked out on you they did exactly what James did to me when I refused to marry him. They confined me in my room, confiscated my clothes so I couldn't find a way to escape, and starved me. I often wonder if it wasn't James's suggestion they do this to me."

"What the hell?"

"He had something on my father. My father worked for him at the time, remember? I think he had been embezzling James's accounts. James was obsessed with me and he told him that if I agreed to marry him he would drop the charges against my father and he wouldn't go to prison and lose everything."

Mark's forehead burrowed into a deep frown as he listened to her story, wishing he could have been there for her instead of nursing his hurt pride because she had turned down his marriage proposal at the time. He would have broken into the house and carried her out and away to safety. The image formed in his mind and he rehearsed the action over and over again as she continued to speak.

"I loved you. I always will and I refused. They stepped up the assault and forced me into a mental institution. They kept me in a private room for a week and drugged me until I was forced to give in."

"I was told you had run away to Europe with him."

She shook her head.

"I married him and we went away for a while. He never had my heart and he was violent. He hated the fact that I still loved you and he couldn't possess me. He brought me back to New York and made sure you were in our social circle so he could flaunt me in front of you. He is so jealous of you, Mark. You don't know what it has been like being forced to keep my distance from you all these years. Every time we saw you he would hit me afterwards and accuse me of having an affair with you. It was awful seeing all those women on your arm. I hated it."

Mark closed his eyes and tightened his arms around her body.

"I will keep you safe from him," he whispered with strength. "I won't let him hurt you ever again. I will not let you down."

She quietly began to sob as he carried her to the bedroom to prepare her for the doctor's examination.

Mark had a quiet word with the young male doctor before he took him into the bedroom to examine Drew.

"I have some other concerns," he quietly informed the man outside the door. "She has been abused by her husband and I believe she might have been raped by him."

"I can do a pelvic exam and, breast check, etc., like we do when you enter a new relationship with a submissive."

Mark nodded. Before embarking on a new relationship as a

dominant he always insisted the woman agree to an intimate medical exam under his watchful eye. That way he could make sure she was healthy inside and out before they played hard together.

"Good."

"Is she already naked and prepared?"

"Yes."

"I will need you to assist me in relaxing the lady," he smiled gently. "As you know, the exam is always easier to perform if the lady is aroused and submissive."

"Of course. We won't have any trouble with her I assure you or she will be disciplined with a spanking. I am very worried about her health and she will do as she is told."

Mark opened the door and the doctor followed him into the room. Drew's long golden curls were trailing like a waterfall over the white sheets, making her look like a captured princess. Every time he saw her, Mark felt his cock twitch and ache to be inside her. The doctor raised his eyes, clearly surprised and enthralled by her beauty. His pupils dilated and a wistful expression suddenly covered his features. Mark smiled to himself, feeling triumphant at the man's admiration of his woman.

The billionaire sat on the bed behind her, helping her up into a sitting position. Nervously, she clutched at the sheet she covered her breasts with. Mark smoothed his fingers up and down her bare arms, trying to soothe her agitation at being naked in front of yet another person in his employ. It would be something she would have to get used to. He liked his women naked most of the time, liked being able to see their soft curves, and it served to keep them obedient and quietly submissive under his control and protection.

The handsome, dark-haired young doctor sat down on the bed in front of her and opened his bag, taking out a stethoscope.

"Let's have a listen to your heart," he spoke softly, gently reaching for the sheet to pull it down and expose her chest. Drew looked alarmed and tried to stop him with her hands. Mark firmly took hold of her arms and pulled her hands away, allowing the man to carefully pull the sheet down to bare her large plump breasts.

"Good girl," he said, lowering the sheet to her waist. "Your breasts appear nice and healthy looking, but I will give them an examination once I have listened to your heart."

Resting a hand on her back as Mark continued to hold her arms open and away from the sheet, the doctor pressed the cool metal end of the stethoscope just underneath her breast to listen to her heart. He finished by listening to her lungs and then moved to place his hands around one free-hanging breast.

Drew whimpered and tried to move away, but he clasped the mound tightly, holding her in place with Mark's assistance.

"Shh, there is nothing to be frightened of. I have examined many breasts," he told her, lifting and lowering the globe to test its weight. Drew whimpered and squirmed again. Smoothing his hands around her flesh he checked for any anomalies before pinching and flexing the dark, plum-colored nipple, stretching it out as far as it would go.

She yelped and struggled, forcing Mark to fight to keep hold of her.

"Drew, allow Aiden to examine your breasts or I will turn you over my knee and spank you," Mark ordered.

Aiden grinned at Mark, who nodded, knowing what was coming next. All of a sudden he raised his hand and slapped her breast. It wobbled and jumped sideways, making Drew gasp in shock. Aiden repeated the action and this time her cry bore an aroused, excited tone she could not suppress.

"Good girl," the doctor cooed, turning his attention to the second milky mound to repeat the process before finishing with another more traditional breast examination. Once he'd finished, Aiden took hold of the sheet around Drew's middle and snatched it away in one quick movement.

Drew cried out desperately, trying to free one of her hands from Mark's hold to cover herself, but Aiden was already moving his fingers gently inside her vagina.

"She is getting wet. Lie her down and we can make her more damp to help me do the pelvic exam."

4

Mark lowered Drew down on the bed and held her there while Aiden pulled away the sheet and tossed it to the floor.

Aiden smiled down at Drew.

"Don't worry, it will be all over soon," he said, patting her thigh.

"Why are you doing this to me?" Drew demanded of the billionaire.

"I have already told you. Hush and be quiet or I will gag you," he scolded.

Aiden took out several instruments from his bag and removed them from their sterile wrappings. Mark curved his hand around one of Drew's breasts to knead it.

"I want you wet for this," he whispered gently. "It will make the examination easier," he coaxed.

His thumb flexed her nipple back and forth and then sharply pinched it and stretched it out. The hot needle of pain that shuddered through the teat gave Drew a curious mix of discomfort and a shiver of pleasure. Mark could see glistening beads of moisture on the neatly shaved curls of her vagina as it began to grow damp and accommodating despite her bashfulness.

Aiden sat down on the bed and covered his hands with a pair of latex gloves. Mark bent to draw her nipple into his mouth expertly, flicking his wet tongue back and forth over, circling the tip around the base as he squeezed the plump round flesh tightly in his hand and harshly suckled at the teat. Drew's eyes glazed and closed as she became lost in Mark's caress—so much so she didn't notice until it was too late when Aiden bent and lifted her bare legs up to her bottom and then splayed them apart. Her eyes flew open. To keep her in place and restrict any movement, Mark clasped his hands around her knees and kept them raised and apart. Unable to move, she had no choice but to surrender herself into the doctor's gentle, capable hands.

"Good, you are getting nice and wet," Aiden stated, using his latex fingers to open Drew's pussy lips wide, stroking his thumbs downward to feel the soft pink flesh and the jewel hanging between them. He drew her clit downward and pinched it lightly. A fresh swell of creamy wetness lathered her vagina.

Convinced she would now keep her legs in place, Mark returned his attention to her breasts. He moved the mounds back and forth in his strong, almost cruel grip while Aiden picked up the steel speculum he was going to use to open up Drew's vagina. Next to him on the bed was a large jar of lubricant. He scooped out a generous amount with his latex fingers and smoothed it over the implement. As he moved to insert the apparatus, Drew decided to move her legs out of position. The doctor shook his head, chuckled, and moved them back. But when she tried it again he surprised her by giving her pussy a sharp slap with his hand. Her body jolted. He did it three more times and Drew became still.

"That's my baby girl," Mark said, gently kissing the top of her forehead. "It will be over soon."

When Aiden inserted the cool steel after pressing down on Drew's legs so that her hips tilted upwards and she was accessible, the speculum slipped easily inside.

Aiden fixed the medical implement in place and peered deep inside Drew's depths with a small torch.

"She looks nice and moist, healthy but I'll take a swab and we can have it tested just to make sure."

Drew gave a small gasp with the gentle movement of the swab inside her channel.

"I'd like to do a bimanual examination as well."

"Proceed," Mark instructed.

Aiden removed the speculum and Drew's body relaxed until he carefully inserted two fingers and stretched them upward toward her uterus. Drew tensed and her legs began to move once more.

"Keep those legs open, Drew," Mark ordered in a severe tone, making her instantly obey him.

"It will be all over very soon." Aiden's voice was soft.

His fingers reached her womb and carefully moved back and forth. He pressed down on her stomach with his hand to judge the health of her uterus and then slowly he moved them away from the organ but did not take his fingers out of Drew's pussy. He pulsed them back and forth, glancing at his employer, who gave him another silent nod of approval.

"All over, little one," Mark reassured. "Time for pleasure."

"Let me see how you perform sexually so I can let Mr. Dexter know your suitability for being a submissive for any more adventurous games he would like to play with you in bed."

Aiden's fingers curled to stroke the rough back wall of her vagina and the center of Drew's pleasure. Mark nipped at the teats of her breasts and feverishly kneaded them back and forth. Aiden picked up his stroke, making Drew pant. The young doctor stared at Drew with lustful, piercing blue eyes as he lowered his mouth to her vagina and lapped greedily, drawing her clit between his teeth.

Drew had opened her mouth to protest but closed it, overcome with need as the man suckled on the droplet and

Mark drew her nipple into his mouth to pinch it with his teeth.

Aiden's strong male palms held Drew's thighs in a vise grip to keep her in place. Her vagina flooded and pooled, filling Aiden's mouth, her orgasm ready to break. Mark kissed her lips, taking her mouth roughly as her hips rose and fell thrusting against Aiden's mouth like a woman possessed. Mark whispered against her lips.

"Wait. I have not given you permission to cum. If you let go before I tell you, you will be spanked."

Panting, Drew fought hard to contain it, but it seemed both men wanted to take her arousal to new heights and test her control by prolonging her torture. She cried and begged and it seemed like an age before the billionaire gave the order for her to climax. It screeched out of her. She bucked against Aiden's face, reaching for her breath, crying and shrieking, unable to stop herself. Mark's hands tightened even harder around her breasts until she believed the imprint of his fingers would be left on her skin. He stared into her eyes capturing her gaze as he and Aiden forced her to ride her pleasure watching every moment it erupted and spurted inside her.

Finally spent, she lay still. Mark kissed her and Aiden lightly brushed her inner thigh with a small kiss. She lay surprised, quiet and satiated until both men released her.

"Now I just want to take your temperature." Doctor Carter's

voice was gentle again. Mark raised Drew to sitting and kept his arm tightly around her, partly for support, partly for restraint. She rested her weary head against his chest and pressed her small, delicate, slender hand into his chest like a child unsure of what was about to unfold, increasing Mark's need to protect her.

"Mark, please drape Drew over your knees face-down."

Drew's eyes widened, comprehending immediately.

"Why can't you just take my temperature in my mouth or under my arm like any other normal doctor?" she snapped.

Doctor Carter grinned at Mark, who was already acting by pulling a struggling naked Drew over his knees.

"It is so I can obtain a more accurate reading and examine your anus," he said standing.

Mark held Drew down over his knees, loving the way her beautiful Titian curls dangled to the floor and her rosy pert bottom lifted high into the air. He circled his fingers over the flesh on one buttock to soothe her while his other palm rested firmly in the middle of her back to keep her still.

The doctor removed his latex gloves to replace them with a new pair and took out a rectal thermometer from his bag. But before inserting it, he approached to give her anus a thorough examination.

He opened the crease of her bottom wide and inspected the

small hole closely. Drew gave a small whimper and shuffled her bottom in a vain effort to retreat from his scrutiny, but the doctor gripped one cheek tightly and raised his other hand to spank the other twice. Shocked, Drew became quiet and still. Mark gave Carter an approving look, which quickly turned into a questioning one.

Doctor Carter carefully pressed on the puckered sides of the orifice and picked up a small torch to look inside Drew's dark channel, frowning before answering Mark's concerned look. After a short while he gave a sigh.

"There is some evidence of old healed tearing," he said quietly.

Mark closed his eyes for a moment, trying to calm the rising tide of anger building inside his body. He wove his fingers through her hair to caress the silky strands.

"Drew, honey, why didn't you tell me he was raping you? Why didn't you run to me? I would have helped you."

Drew was silent as Aiden moved away to pick up the jar of lubricant and get the thermometer ready for insertion.

There was emotion in Drew's voice when she spoke.

"I tried to. Every time I tried to run he hunted me down and dragged me back just like he did last week. He always told me he would kill you if I went near you. Do you remember those death threats you received last month and the car that nearly ran you down? And the way the police couldn't find out who they were from? They were paid off. It was him, Mark. It was a warning for me as well. That is why I kept away. I couldn't lose you. He is consumed with jealousy over you. He knows I still love you and he hates it."

"Fuck. I am going to kill him."

"Mark, hold her for me," Aiden requested with a sympathetic look, giving him something to concentrate on to keep his cool.

Aiden dipped his middle finger into the jar of lubricant once more and thickly coated it. He opened the crease between Drew's buttocks and trailed his fingers around her anal opening. Drew shivered on top of Mark's knees, feeling the odd sensation of the moist cool gel in an intimate region of her body. She jumped a little and tried to lift her body up when Aiden slowly probed his finger into the opening and thrusted gently inside.

"Mark, help me out. You know what to do."

Mark nodded and slipped one of his fingers underneath Drew's pelvis and sank his fingers into Drew's pussy. She was still nice and wet. Softly he stroked until he could hear her cries turn into moans and her body relaxed its tense appearance over his knees. He inserted his own middle finger inside her pussy and began to pump it slowly in and out of her, teasing the velvet muscles inside her channel with his expert stroke to distract her as Aiden examined her further, then removed his finger.

"Stay nice and relaxed for me, Drew. I am going to take your temperature now. Stay very still."

Mark took his cue and stilled his finger inside her pussy, allowing her to simply feel the strength and reassurance of his presence and penetration.

With his fingers on either side, Aiden held Drew's butt cheeks apart and looked inside the small puckered crevice before inserting the cool tip of the rectal thermometer he'd thickly lubricated. It started to tense. Drew attempted to shuffle a little, prompting Mark to press his palm down harder on her back to hold her in place.

The invasion was odd. The end of the medical apparatus was uncomfortable as it traveled along her channel, and the urge to wriggle and expel it was overwhelming. Doctor Carter buried the long thermometer as far as it would go and then allowed Drew's bottom to close around it. He twisted the end and tapped a buttock, making her squirm.

"Well done. It won't take long to get a reading."

Mark bent his lips to brush the small of Drew's back in a line down to her bottom.

"You are safe now, darling. No one is going to hurt you again now that you are with me. I will make him pay for all he has done to you. I will never forgive myself for not being there for you."

"Please, Mark. You can't blame yourself. There was no other way."

The thermometer beeped, causing Mark to lift his head. Aiden approached again and slowly removed the thermometer from her anus. He stared at it for a moment and then smiled.

"Good. All fine," he said, snapping off his gloves.

Mark started to move his finger again, stepping up the pace of his thrusts.

"Good girl. You've done well."

He knew Drew would be sensitive after both Aiden's and his own manipulation of her body and he was pleased when she suddenly gasped and came relatively quickly, allowing him to enjoy the feel of her silky muscles tightly gripping his finger as though to milk seed from it.

The billionaire covered Drew with the sheet again after Aiden had made some other checks and asked her a couple of questions. He kissed her.

"Get some more rest and when you wake you can eat. My chef is preparing a meal for you."

Satisfied when she closed her eyes and snuggled down on the pillow, Mark left her and followed the doctor outside.

"There was some old scarring, Mr. Dexter, so I have to conclude Ms. Sumner has been raped by her husband in the past. She is also suffering from exhaustion and some symptoms of malnutrition. That explains the dizzy symptoms.

She is weak and under tremendous emotional stress with the disappearance of her child. It is vital she gets a lot of rest to get her strength back. Confine her to bed for a few days while she starts eating again and gets her strength back, then no strenuous activity for a couple of weeks until she gets back on her feet. She is more than suitable for submission play, but keep it gentle for a while until she is well and gains more confidence and trust in you."

"I will. Thank you."

The billionaire saw the man out and then decided to make a visit to James Sumner while Drew slept to make his feelings known and mark his territory over Drew.

5

Mark stepped out of the lift on the 51st floor of Sumner INC. He hadn't been expected to be allowed into the building, let alone shown to the lift that would take him directly up to Sumner's office. Seemed his enemy wanted to have a discussion about Drew as much as he did.

His fist clenched and unclenched at his side, itching to land Sumner a beating for raping Drew. Her life must have been torture. Since she'd told him, all he could do was vividly imagine what the man had done to her. All so she could protect his life. The images taunted him and refused to leave his mind. He had to keep breathing deeply just to keep his temper in control. But his heart was beating fast with his anger so much, he thought it might burst when he stepped out of the lift outside Sumner's office. It propelled him forward.

Ignoring the request of Sumner's secretary who welcomed him to take a seat and wait to be called in, he crossed the room and brushed her aside. He threw open Sumner's door and strode into it without apology.

James Sumner was fair and only two years older than Mark Dexter's thirty-five. He was handsome. There was no point in denying it, but he did not have the striking dark features or height of his nemesis.

The two men sitting in the red and gilt chairs in front of the man's excessively elaborate cream marble desk trimmed with heavy gilt on the edges and legs stood up disturbed and confused by the interruption. Mark grimaced at the desk. Since James had gained wealth his need to be ostentatious knew no bounds. The whole large office was filled with clutter in the form of antiques and was dripping in gold and marble. The idiot had no idea of style.

"Ah, Mark. I have been waiting for you to arrive," he paused to laugh. "Ever the dramatic. You and I need to have a chat about that pretty little piece of my property you appear to have appropriated for yourself," he said with biting bitterness, standing and turning to face Mark approaching him from the side.

But Mark was already around the desk, pulling him out of his chair to hit him square on the jaw with a hard, unforgiving punch. It sent James sprawling backward onto his chair, scraping his throne sideways across the floor. He slumped down onto the floor at its feet.

"Sir," Sumner's secretary was shocked, her hand over her mouth. "I've called security. They are on their way."

"Rapist," Mark hissed.

Sumner laughed and nursed his mouth, wiping at the blood dripping from it.

"No security, Maya. Send them away. Everyone leave. I need to talk to Mark alone."

"But Sir," one of the men was protesting, approaching Mark in an aggressive stance.

"I said leave. I assure you I can more than look after myself. He just caught me off-guard. Now leave or you are all fired. Do I make myself clear?" he bellowed.

"Yes, Sir," they all mumbled, leaving the room.

Mark stood breathing hard, waiting for the door to close behind them so he could go for Sumner again. The moment it did he lunged for Sumner, who was still sitting on the floor wiping at his mouth. He laughed as Mark pulled him to his feet by the lapels of his suit jacket. Mark punched him in the stomach, making him grunt.

"This is just like old times in the Brotherhood, Mark," he laughed, trying to catch his breath. Mark frowned at him. "Fighting over the same girl. What's it like to be on the losing side this time?"

Mark pushed him backward and slammed him against the wall, wondering why the hell he wasn't fighting back. He just appeared to be enjoying the show and letting Mark get it out of his system. He thought he held all the cards no matter what Mark did to him, and it both confused and worried the billionaire.

"I haven't lost. She belongs to me now. She is not Leila. Leila died. She was murdered, remember? By our rival gang, the Toms. We both lost that day. There was no winner."

For the first time since Drew had told him what had happened the violent images were interrupted in his mind and instead a memory of the day Leila died played. He could still see the car as clearly as though it passed him now in the office, the gun poking out as it fired and shot Leila dead in front of them both in a drive-by shooting. He would never forget watching the confused expression on her face as her pretty small curved body turned and flopped onto the ground like a rag doll. She was only nineteen when she died, only a year younger than himself at the time. It had been a clear shot to the head and she had been killed instantly. It made him all the more protective of Drew.

For a moment Sumner was silent and he bent his head. Mark wondered if he was reliving the same memory.

"Maybe not," Sumner said, recovering. "But Drew is mine. Give her back. If you don't you are putting her in more danger than you realize."

"You are never getting her back. You raped her."

Mark hit his stomach again.

"She won't get Eva back if she stays with you."

"I am going to make sure she presses charges against you for kidnap, rape, and domestic violence. I am already looking for Eva and when I find her she will live under my roof with her mother and I will adopt her as my own."

James's face turned a dark shade of crimson and finally the

monster that Mark knew lurked deep inside showed itself. He fought back, catching Mark in the stomach. He was quickly forced to block a punch to his face before he was able to slam James back against the wall again and trap him there.

"Give Eva back. I have already alerted the police."

"I know. They have been here. I've told them she is with relatives on holiday because Drew is unwell with mental health problems and as a result she is an unfit mother. They were ready to believe my little tale."

"Fucking bastard."

"She needs to come back to me, Mark. She needs to toe the line and stop investigating for that damn article she is writing for The New York Times before she gets us both killed."

Mark's heart swelled with pride. Drew was writing again. An excellent investigative journalist, she hadn't written a word since she'd married Sumner. He'd never taken her for the stay-at-home good little wife. His suspicions about James preventing her were now confirmed.

"What is she writing about?"

"She hasn't told you?" Sumner shook his head. "Devious journalist to the last. She is writing a piece on your estranged English father, Lewis Dexter. One of her friends' daughters came to her with the story. He is trafficking women through Europe as sex slaves to Arab terrorists. You have to admire the man for creating such a lucrative business. The daughter had been kidnapped for sale but escaped and the woman wants Drew to help her find her. The police have no leads. Your father always manages to cover his back. Drew connected the dots and won't let it rest until she brings him down. You know what she is like when on a story. I had to send Eva away to force her to stop."

"My God, you are working with my father. He's paid you off and offered you a cut."

"Business is business, Mark. You know that. It comes in many forms. Part of the deal is Drew's silence. If I can't control her, they will kill her."

Mark punched his face again.

"Like father, like son."

Mark's black eyes narrowed sharply at the glee in Sumner's eyes. He always knew how to push his buttons. The hit knocked Sumner sideways and the billionaire let him fall to the floor.

"You are scum and I won't let you get away with this. Keep away from Drew or you are a dead man." He pointed at him on the floor before turning on his heel to stride out of the office.

Mark hurried back to his apartment, conscious Drew was in danger if he wasn't with her. He had to stop her writing the story. There had to be another way to solve the problem without putting the woman he loved at any more risk. But when he returned he found Drew gone.

"Where the hell has she gone? She is going to get herself killed. I need her back home and safe now!" Mark shouted at Tomas. "How the hell did she get past security?"

"No one knows. You know how resourceful she is as a journalist. I think she is trying to leave the country. She could be anywhere."

"It has to be Italy. James has an Italian aunt living in Venice. He told the police Eva was with relatives. They were close when he was a teenager and she lived in New York. He might have given Eva to her to hide. She has never liked Drew and has always wanted a child she couldn't have. She dotes on James and would do anything for him. Widen your search for the child outside of the country," he instructed, running his hands thorough his raven hair as he paced the room frantically trying to work out where Drew would have gone. It wasn't just James Sumner who was after her now, but somebody far worse—his father.

"What about your twin brother in the UK? He has the resources to find her quickly. Doesn't he work for that international intelligence organization Interdefense or something? I know you won't like it, but I recommend you contact him. He is your only hope of reaching Drew before your father does. Swallow your pride and the argument of who your mother loved the most and for fuck's sake, call him."

Mark stared at Tomas, realizing he was right. He didn't like it but he had no choice. He flopped down on his leather chair behind his desk.

"Get my twin Dylan on the phone and put the call through to me the minute you make contact."

6

Interdefense Sub Station, London

The young woman heaved and tested her bindings on the bed. She was completely naked. Her breasts were flat against the bedcovers and her bare bottom was raised to prominence. The girl's arms stretched between her kneeling legs and were fixed in leather cuffs attached to a spreader bar binding her ankles next to them. As a result, the crease between her buttocks was forced to open, exposing the vulnerable dark puckered hole for penetration. It also provided a tantalizing glimpse of her ripe vulva. She wore a blindfold over her eyes and quietly she whimpered.

The bed was the only object in the small room. A solitary tall man in an immaculate dark grey designer suit stood in the shadows of the dimly lit space stood over her. In his hand he held a curled leather bullwhip ready to extract the information he needed from the imprisoned woman in the cell. It was time to begin her interrogation.

Dylan Dexter rested his large manicured palm on the girl's bottom and stroked it lovingly. He peered into her small anal hole, trying to judge its size for the object he was to insert. The girl had proved difficult to interrogate, stubbornly refusing to tell him of her boyfriend's whereabouts and where he planned to kill the government minister. An environmental activist who was prepared to kill rather than achieve his objectives in a peaceful manner and the luck of the Devil in avoiding the authorities, Dylan believed the only way to find Jonas was through his girlfriend and he'd picked her up that afternoon.

She'd proved a handful and resisted arrest. He'd tackled her to the floor of the kitchen after she'd thrown several pots and pans at him and dragged her hands behind her back. That was when she turned and bit his wrist. Grimacing with blood staining his white cuff, he decided to show her he meant business. Pulling her up off the floor with one hand holding her wrists together behind her back and the other tugging her long dark ponytail, he had raised her from the kitchen floor and slammed her frontways against the wall. Making sure her pretty face didn't smack the wall, he pulled harder on the ponytail until her head stretched uncomfortably back.

"Where is he?" Dylan demanded, pulling her hair hard.

"I am not telling you anything!" she screamed at him.

He couldn't help but laugh.

"Oh, you will by the time I am finished with you."

He frowned down at the blood seeping from his wound and staining his cuff. The shirt was ruined.

The girl was wearing a short dress and as Dylan thought of his ruined shirt and the throbbing pain coming from his wrist, he ached to spank her backside. The quick flash of her white thong as he slammed her against the wall again, exposing her partially bare bottom, was too inviting not to smack. To calm her, he let go of her hair and lifted the cotton strappy white summer dress to her waist and bunched it there. She squealed and fought, but his lean, athletic frame was far too strong. With lightning speed, he moved his fingers down inside the top of her thong, just above the covered crease between her buttocks. In one motion, he pulled it down over her bottom.

Two juicy plump pale globes bounced free from the restraining hold the thong had placed around it. Admiring their pertness, the spy pulled the thong down over her thighs, snapping the delicate straps at the side until the flimsy material came away in his hands. He tossed it to the floor and cupped the side of her rump.

"Open your legs," he commanded, squeezing her rump painfully tight.

When she refused, he bent his head to examine her pouting vagina. Slipping his deft fingers between her thighs, he found the small bud protruding from her labia and squeezed it. She gasped and a tell-tale trickle of moisture sluiced his fingers, making him grin. So the suspect liked to be firmly handled. He raised his hand and softly curved it before spanking her pussy hard to encourage her to move, careful to catch the tip of the clit.

The girl yelped and he repeated the action and his order.

"Open your legs, now."

The second whip of his palm across her vulva, a little harder this time, induced her to spread her legs.

"Move away from the wall and bend over."

Now that her legs were open, it was difficult for her to move and it would keep her restrained. With his help, she managed to move away from the wall but she refused to bend over and he was forced to slap her pussy one more time. She obeyed quickly and when he removed his hand he could see it was damp with arousal.

Holding her hands behind her back, Dylan decided she was ready for the first part of her interrogation, a spanking.

"I don't like being bitten, Gemma. Nor do I like getting blood on my shirt. You deserve to be taken to task for it," he told her with humor.

"You are going to spank me like a child," she retorted.

"Yes. I am."

"What? Ow."

He delivered the first slap to the right buttock, enjoying the way it jumped and quivered with the force he used. He struck the left just a touch harder, making her howl before picking up the pace.

"Where is Jonas?" Dylan demanded above the sound of her flesh being smacked echoing around the small room.

He stood over her curved form strongly spanking her bare bottom, each blow reddening her buttocks until they burned and stung. Each strike lifted her blushed bottom into the air with increasing force when she refused to answer him.

"We will find him. If you tell me now I can save his life. Do you want him to die, Gemma? I thought you loved him."

Another slap rained down upon her, this time on the tender backs of her thighs. Dylan had noticed she had been biting her lip to steel herself but now she opened her mouth and let out a loud sob. The tears she had been defiantly holding back spilled from her eyes to run in a torrent down her cheeks.

"I won't tell you," she shouted.

Dylan whipped his hand neatly across the back of one thigh, making her howl like a baby.

"But you know where he is. That's a start."

"He is going to kill that man and stop the animal experimentation. People will listen then."

"Tell me where he is."

Dylan glanced down at her red thighs and bottom. She wasn't giving anything up yet and it appeared she needed further persuasion of a firmer kind. If he continued to spank her he wouldn't be able to apply any other method to interrogate her. He wasn't a cruel man, only when he needed to be.

The spy gave his prisoner one more slap across her bottom and ended her spanking. For his own curiosity, he moved his hand across her sex and to his satisfaction found her soaking wet. Despite her cries of pain, the woman was deeply aroused by her punishment. He could use this to his advantage.

Laying his palm on her flesh, he rubbed one mound to soothe the burning.

"I am going to take you in and we are going to discuss this further," he told her. "You will tell me. It is just a matter of time."

He ignored her cursing and lowered her arms, keeping hold of one. Quickly he dipped his tall frame and lifted her neatly over his shoulder, preventing her fist from making contact with his face.

The spy had carried his prisoner to the car half-naked. The act was designed to weaken her will. Neighbors looked out of their windows and up from their gardening, shocked to see her fiery-red bottom on public display. He was satisfied when she began to whimper with her embarrassment.

Depositing her in the back of the car, he leaned over her and took hold of the dress at the front to brutally tear and rip it from her body. To his surprise, the girl barely protested and as he stripped her naked she let out a pleasured gasp.

The man sitting in the driver's seat grinned and turned around to admire Dexter's handiwork, sweeping his eyes over the prisoner's voluptuous naked breasts as Dylan undid the catch of the girl's bra and pulled it down her arms, allowing them to bob free from their confinement.

"Did she talk?" the man asked him.

"No, but she will."

"I love watching you work," he grinned again.

"Spread your legs, Gemma," Dylan ordered, giving her large breasts a couple of expert slaps to encourage her obedience. She took a breath and arched her body forward to meet the third quick strike to her left breast, apparently eager for more chastisement. Dylan smiled to himself. He had her just where he wanted. Aroused and pliant. He would manipulate this to his advantage in the interrogation. As if to prolong the punishment, she kept her legs closed, prompting another slap. Dylan watched her breast flush with the strike and wobble deliciously from side to side.

"That girl needs a pussy whipping," the driver encouraged. "She will learn to be obedient at the center. Let's go."

Dylan decided to oblige his colleague. Quickly he cupped Gemma's sex and squeezed it hard and then pushed the lips together tightly. He did it once more, making her moan as the pink fleshy wet mounds rubbed against each other. Involuntarily she opened her legs, taken with the pleasure and unable to help herself. The moment she spread her legs, Dylan raised his hand and whipped her sex with his palm four times hard. The girl never closed her legs again.

His hand was wet with her creamy juice when he moved it away to place her hands behind her back and the seatbelt between her blushed breasts. He'd sat in the back of the car as it drove through the London traffic, watching the way she rubbed her wet pussy across the black leather, dampening it to ease the ache dwelling in her sex. Her labial lips were heavy and swollen and her nipples were tautly erect. His fingers twitched to stroke her damp vulva, to play a little, but he remained still and cold until the car dipped down the ramp to the underground building in Interdefense's London office. Loosening her seatbelt, he'd pulled her back over his shoulder and carried her into the building and straight to one of the interrogation cells where he'd arranged her in the spreader bar.

It was his first intention to take the bullwhip to her bottom after she'd still refused to answer his questions, but now he believed a stronger method was needed. Convinced of the correct size of plug he would need to use to fit in her exposed anus, he put down the whip and covered his hands in a pair of latex gloves before coating his middle finger in lubricant. Time to get her stretched.

Dylan plied open her buttocks a little more so that the girl felt uncomfortable. Holding the cheeks painfully spread, he circled his wet finger around her hole. The girl cried. The hole appeared tight and virginal.

"Please, what are you doing?" she panted with anxiety.

"A quick examination of your anus. Has a man ever taken you here?"

"No. I've never…"

"Then this will be a new experience for you. If you don't want me to proceed, tell me where Jonas is."

His English voice was formal and perfect in its delivery of the threat and more than adequately sinister.

"No."

Dylan didn't ask her anymore. He circled the dark puckered entrance, thickly sluicing it with lubricant. Then he began to ease his middle finger into the tight hole. The girl gasped but said nothing. He felt her frame tighten and rubbed his latex hand over one globe as though to soothe and eased his finger in deeper, forcing the walls of her anus to stretch and accommodate his invasion. Again she whimpered but said nothing, allowing him to go further. He wasn't quite at the hilt but with a sudden sharp wet thrust he embedded his finger, making her body jolt on the bar. The cry she gave was of surprise but was also tinged with a renewed arousal.

Dylan simply held his finger there for a moment, allowing her to get used to his dominance, guiding her into surrender, but the girl was stubborn and remained silent. With a tinge of cruelty, he began to thrust his finger in and out of her body, forcing the channel to stretch and widen to accommodate the enema tubing and the plug he would insert to force her to hold the warm water he pumped into her stomach.

"OK, Gemma, you leave me no choice."

Dylan removed his finger quickly, brushing her sex to check if she had dampened further and found that she had. She was a natural submissive and was obviously used to a firm hand from Jonas. He needed to push her boundaries. Anal penetration was the best way to start, and he was doubtful she had experienced the dual pleasure/pain of an enema. It could be her undoing.

He turned to the large mirror in the room, knowing his colleagues were behind it viewing the whole interrogation.

"Prepare an enema," he instructed, removing his gloves with a snapping motion.

Gemma cried.

"No, please."

Dylan leaned over her and softly cupped his hand over her sex from behind. Once more he squeezed it and caressed the small bud, kneading it between his fingers, tugging it back and forth until her cries turned into moans.

"Have you ever had an enema before, Gemma?" he asked gently.

"No."

"Well, I insert a tube into your bottom. The warm water flows along the tube into your anus and through to your stomach. Your abdomen will swell with water until you feel as though you are carrying a child full term. Then the pain will start.

Some women are deeply aroused by the pain when they are made to hold the water inside their body for a while. Others beg for release. I like to plug the anus to force the person to retain the fluid. I wonder how long I can force you to endure the discomfort before you tell me of Jonas's whereabouts," he told her in a dark whisper.

He only heard small cries of fear in between the moans as he continued to caress her pussy, teasing her by circling the entrance of her channel but never penetrating it with his finger.

"Please don't."

"Tell me where he is."

"I can't. I can't betray him."

"Yes you can. He is a murderer. You aren't. Do you want to spend the rest of your life in jail for helping him?"

"No."

"Then tell me where he is," Dylan persisted, keeping a tight rein on his impatience.

"I can't," she suddenly sobbed.

"Then you will take the enema," he said, glancing up at a man bringing the prepared enema into the room and a stand to hold the bag. "When your stomach is cramping you will want to tell me."

Dylan put on a fresh pair of latex gloves and coated his fingers in the lubricant once more along with the end of the tube. The girl sobbed as he prepared it. Taking the tube from the assistant, he stretched open the small anal hole and began feeding the tube into her bottom. She moaned and bucked her bottom backwards in an attempt to expel the tube, making Dylan increase the speed with which he used to push it inside her. Holding her down with one hand to keep her in place, the spy turned the valve on the tube to allow the water to flow from the soft plastic holder resembling a small hot water bottle hooked on a stand like a drip.

The water coursed fast along the tube up inside her anus into the girl's stomach to flood her colon and begin the cleansing process. She gasped, feeling the warm water begin to fill her insides. Dylan loved giving enemas to a submissive woman. It was the ultimate way to dominate her. He slipped his hands between her legs and up to her stomach, intoxicated by the way it was swelling and enlarging into his palm. She was completely in his power. He lightly caressed the surface.

"Good girl, take it all," he cooed.

Eventually he determined she had taken sufficient water and turned off the valve. His assistant had gloved his hands and handed him a steel butt plug lathered in lubricant. It was large and would pull open the small entrance, causing Gemma to experience a new sense of discomfort and to feel unbearably full. He wondered if it would bring more pleasure for her.

Dylan pressed the cool tip of the plug at Gemma's anal

entrance and circled it, allowing her to anticipate the insertion. She bleated a little but still did not answer his question about Jonas. Dylan carefully penetrated her entrance with the plug and pushed it inside. She moaned and tried to rear again but he persisted, watching the small hole stretch and widen to accept it. When the plug was deeply embedded, he stood back and took off his gloves. Gemma was beginning to groan with pain. The cramps from the fluid had come quickly. It was time to get the information he needed.

The assistant left the room and Dylan scraped a solitary chair across the floor to the bottom end of the bed to face Gemma's bottom. He sat down and waited.

"Those cramps are only going to increase, Gemma," he said in a matter-of-fact crisp English tone, watching her move restlessly on her bindings in a futile attempt to free herself. "You will endure them until you give me the information I need."

"I can't betray him."

"Why not? He doesn't care for you, Gemma. He isn't here trying to rescue you. He is probably in bed with one of the many women he fucks every night while you wait at home for him. We know he likes to fuck when he's killed someone. It was the first thing he did when he murdered that girl who crossed him. He isn't a fighter for your cause. He has form and he likes the thrill of killing. He is going to kill Paul Strand for the leader of your group for money. He is just a hired assassin. He has been fooling you that he cares about your cause."

"You are lying."

"You know I'm not. You've been fooling yourself because you love him."

"Please, I have to go to the bathroom and release this water."

"No, you can't. Hold it."

"I can't."

"Then tell me where Jonas is."

"Please!" she screamed.

Dylan stood and held her stomach again, pressing it down to increase her discomfort. At the same time his free hand pressed down on the plug. The girl sobbed uncontrollably.

"Tell me."

The girl moved from side to side. Dylan pressed harder as she cried out.

"He is at a flat in Tremayne Street preparing to shoot the minister when he makes his speech in the guild hall tonight about the medical advancement of the new cancer drug."

"What number?"

"Forty-four. Now please."

"Not yet. You've been a good girl," he said, moving his hand from her stomach to her pussy to stroke her clit allowing pleasure to war with the cramp for supremacy in her mind. "You deserve a reward."

Dylan glanced at the mirror and nodded, knowing agents would have already been sent to arrest Jonas the moment the girl gave the information. He inserted his finger inside her heavily damp pussy and pulsed it in and out. Her cries turned to helplessly confused moans. Now she was plugged in every orifice apart from her mouth. Feeling her begin to buck down onto his finger, he curled it inside her velvet soft channel until it hit the rough back wall of her vagina and forced her orgasm to erupt. Rocking on his fingers, whimpering and sobbing while trapped in the pleasure/pain paradox, the prisoner came hard to Dylan's satisfaction. As soon as her exhausted, tortured pants ended, he undid her wrists and ankles. Carefully he allowed her to sit up and called for an assistant to take her to the bathroom.

He smiled when his superior, Tina Andrews, came into the room.

"Well done."

Dylan nodded with respect and walked to the sink on the other side of the room away from the mirror to wash his hands.

"I have another job for you in Venice. But first you need to take a call from your brother in New York. He's pulled a lot of strings to find you here." Dylan frowned and shook his head as he dried his hands with a towel.

She put her hand up to stop him speaking when he opened his mouth to object.

"He has a problem and I have a feeling it is linked to one of ours. I know you don't want to speak to him or have anything to do with him, but I need you to put your differences aside and pump him for information that can help us. I have sent you details."

Dylan put his suit jacket back on.

"He won't be able to help us. This is a waste of time."

"I disagree. Try it."

7

If he let her out of his sight she was a dead woman. It was hard to achieve his optimum speed weaving through the slow-moving crowds of tourists littering the small narrow streets of Venice on a hot July day, but Dylan moved skilfully, never taking his eyes off her for one second.

She was being pursued up the steps of the Rialto Bridge by two men. There was no question of their intent. They meant to kill her but neither of them could achieve a clean shot. The objective would be to get up close with a silencer and execute the takedown with a shot to the back of the head. The woman would fall dead and they would simply disappear into the crowd. He watched one of the assailants lower a weapon to his side as he slipped between two couples to pick up speed.

The man carrying the silencer put his hand on the red-haired woman's shoulder and pulled her back against him just as Dylan pounced and yanked him back hard. She turned around shrieking with fright, nearly losing her balance on the steps.

"Keep running," he shouted, grabbing the man's hand holding the weapon and twisting it around, banging down hard on his arm to force him to drop it. For a moment she stared at him confused.

"Mark?" she questioned.

"Run."

Someone in the crowd cried out as they were shoved, caught in the middle of the fight. The gun fell to the ground and clattered down the steps, making people jump out of the way to avoid it.

The crowd of disturbed tourists dispersed quickly, giving Dylan room to swing the man around and push him between the shop stalls toward the wall of the bridge. The man squirmed in Dylan's hold, using all of his strength trying to force his captor backwards but the agent's movements were quick and methodical and the assailant's actions proved futile. Dylan moved his legs around the man's with calculated precision. The attacker lost his balance and fell back against the wall. Without hesitation Dylan used the momentum to tip him backward over the wall and down over the bridge into the canal.

He didn't wait to hear the splash. Placing his grey and silver tie back inside his suit jacket, he moved through the crowd watching the man thrash about in the Grand Canal below and took off after the woman again. Moving through the people gasping and looking down at him thrashing about in the water, the suited man returned to pick up the silencer and took off after the girl again. Time was short and he had to get to her before the second hitman got to her.

Tucking the weapon inside his suit jacket, he ran down the steps unhindered by dithering tourists. This time they were all desperate to keep out of his way. The woman wasn't visible at first when he submerged himself in the cramped thin streets running alongside the canals. Then he spotted her short poppy red mac weaving in and out of the holidaymakers. She turned to see the man who was chasing her. He was holding something in his hand. It wasn't a gun but a knife this time. Dylan couldn't see the woman's eyes because they were covered by her dark sunglasses just like his own, but he knew enough details from the dossier he'd been given on her that they were blue. Her head kept turning back to see her attacker as Dylan gained ground. The assailant was far too close for comfort, and Dylan could sense anytime now he was going to jump her.

Something must have snapped inside, because the small curvy redhead surprised him, stopping and turning to make a stand as the man came at her. She took off the bag slung over her body and swung it hard in his face. She used all of her strength to push him backward to make him fall over. It was enough to let Dylan catch them up.

Her pursuer pointed his blade at her and tried to ram it into her stomach. The knife thrust through her soft summer mac, slashing her across her middle and drawing blood. Then he drew it across her arm as she bent to clutch at her stomach wound. She tried to dodge being knifed again, but the man swiped the blade across her side. From the small distance separating them Dylan could see it hadn't gone in because she had moved and stopped the man from having a chance to really plunge the knife into her.

Fueled by adrenaline, she lashed out at the man with a punch. She missed and groaned heavily with pain from the wound. People around them were shouting for the police and two men tried to approach the knife-wielding man from behind, but Dylan grabbed their arms and pulled them back.

"Police. Get back," he instructed in fluent Italian.

As the man tried to kill the Interdefense agent's charge once more, Dylan wound his arm around the hitman's neck in an arm lock and dragged him backward away from her. The attacker swung his arm, wildly jabbing the knife at Dylan while the woman replaced her fallen bag on her injured body and looked on, panting to get her breath and clutching her lightly bleeding stomach wound. After successfully avoiding the knife penetrating his side by twisting his body, Dylan tightened his square jaw and turned the man's head quickly to one side with precision movement, cleanly snapping his neck. He coldly dropped the dead body and stepped over it to get to the girl.

She stared at him with disbelief, then her face turned green and for a moment Dylan was sure she was going to vomit. Everyone had kept their distance, doing all they could to leave the street. He dragged the body into a dark corner undetected and slumped it against the wall, hearing the whistles of the police as they made their way through the streets toward them.

The woman started to back away as Dylan walked toward her with purpose. He swiftly glanced at the wounds to her stomach and arm, quickly assessing their severity. They were small flesh wounds. She'd done well to stop the man from plunging the knife in deep. It could have been a lot worse. Having no time to argue, he roughly grabbed her arm in a tight grip and propelled her forward. They had to get away before the police arrived. This was a covert operation with no involvement from the local enforcement or the agency which Interdefense secretly operated under, Interpol. Any interference would put the mission at risk and end the woman's life, which was to be avoided at all costs. She was far too important a witness to lose.

The police were getting closer. Dylan swung her by the arm into another of the less traveled streets full of rundown buildings and graffiti and forced her back against the doorway of a small café. With an arm above her head and his hand tight around her waist, he pressed close to her body to shield her from view as the Carabinieri passed by. An intoxicating smell of peach and jasmine filled his nostrils. She was a beautiful woman and even in the moment of danger he couldn't help but notice it being this close to her small, fragile form. His brother had chosen well. She questioned him again in a whisper.

"Mark, what are you doing here? How…"

Dylan put a finger to his lips, motioning for her to be silent.

"I'm not Mark. I am Dylan, his identical twin. Hush."

She said no more and just stared at him in disbelief.

Drew was panting, pressing her hands into wall trying to keep a discreet distance from him while eyeing her rescuer with suspicion and caution. Believing she was safe when she heard the police pass by at the top end of the short enclosed street, she attempted to move away but Dylan held her fast, banging her back against the wall and closing his hand around her throat to hold her in place.

"Don't move until I tell you," he snapped, listening to the footsteps of the tourists, knowing instinctively that by the slow tread of one of them another assailant was walking down the alleyway looking for them. He moved away from her and looked out.

He thought it wasn't the police but another of the men sent to kill her. He drew his own weapon, a semi-automatic Glock 17 from the holster in his suit jacket, and outstretching his arm he pushed the woman further back into the doorway behind him, warning her to stay put with his narrowed black eyes.

Moving out from the doorway, he raised his weapon and pointed it straight at the man.

"Who sent you? Lewis Dexter?" Dylan demanded in a cool, collected voice.

The man grinned.

"None of your fucking business," he said in English with an Italian accent. "Where is the girl?"

"None of your fucking business," Dylan told him eloquently, shooting him dead before the killer could pull the trigger.

The bullet sliced into the man's forehead and embedded itself in his brain, killing him instantly.

Unflinching as though he were an automaton, Dylan turned back to the doorway. The journalist and his brother's lover he had been sent to protect were paling. He quickly loosened her mac, ignoring her protests, and lifted up the thin black camisole she wore underneath to expose her injuries. Gently he placed his hands on either side of the slashes and bent to examine them. He was right; they were superficial like the one on her arm, but she needed a doctor to stitch them up.

"You'll live," he reassured her, dropping the top back down.

"I never knew Mark had a brother, let alone an identical twin. You look so alike. I can't tell any difference. Why are you here? Are you police or something? You just killed that man."

She struggled as he reached for her uninjured arm and dragged her out of the doorway.

"Not now. We have to move fast."

Her movement had slowed. She looked exhausted and as they rushed through the streets to reach the nearest canal to take a water taxi to the safe house he'd been instructed to transport her to, Dylan felt her body slumping against him. She was slowing them down. He stopped suddenly to swing the girl around and dipped his body, pulling her neatly over his shoulder and began to run.

Dylan had memorized every detail of Venice and he knew the escape route he had devised well.

A water taxi was pulling up at a jetty on the inner canal to unload passengers who were rushing up the waterlogged stone steps. He let them pass and began walking down the wet, algae-covered steps. The worried looks he was receiving at the woman strewn over his shoulder like a slain deer bleeding down his suit from people in gondolas on the canal and around him did nothing to distract him from his mission. He carried the journalist down to the boat, pulling out the Glock once more. He aimed it at the water taxi's driver.

"Are you going to help us and earn a lot of money or do I have to make you?" he demanded in Italian.

The driver raised his dark bushy eyebrows as he stared at the Glock and then at his male companion. He grinned, undeterred.

"I have no problem earning money whatever the reason."

He motioned for them to come aboard. Dylan felt Drew fall limp and unconscious over his shoulder just as he jumped from the step into the boat.

8

Drew lay naked on the bed asleep, having been sedated by the doctor. She was due to wake any moment. Her arms were now raised above her head with her wrists restrained in black leather cuffs that were tied to the bed by a leather strap fed through a loop down the back of the bed. Her feet were in a similar position and tied together. Dylan viewed her with approval, giving her light wounds that had been stapled a quick check. His staff in the safe house located on a private island near Murano away from the city had carried out his directions for her confinement to the letter. She needed to be interrogated for the information she carried on his father and his trafficking operation.

Mark wouldn't approve of his actions, but he was now in charge of Drew's care and safety. And it was vital he found out as much as he could from her to enable him to effectively protect her and help her get her child back. This was the chance he had been waiting for to bring his father down and prevent an escalation in his criminal activities across Europe. Besides, Mark had told him she had managed to find a way past his security. She wouldn't be doing that with him. Keeping her naked and bound would ensure she wouldn't be going anywhere.

He stood over her, sweeping his eyes over her small curved form with appreciation. She was very beautiful and tempting.

The ache to touch her and trace every soft swell and curve with his fingertips was strong. But she didn't belong to him. Not that it had ever stopped him before. What the hell was she doing with his arrogant prick of a twin brother?

She turned on her bindings onto her side, giving him a delicious view of her rosy pink spanked bottom. He chuckled knowing his brother's penchant for applying a swift bare bottom spanking to any woman in his care who required firm discipline. Unable to help himself, Dylan softly cupped a cheek with his hand and stroked her skin, imagining her over his own knees with his hand slapping at her rump.

The cuff of his white shirt caressed her side as he positioned his arm over her and gently gathered up one of her breasts in his hand. Seductively, almost lovingly, he squeezed it to wake her, flexing his thumb across the nipple. She stirred, but it took a firmer squeeze to rouse her from slumber.

"Drew, I need you to wake up now. We have to talk," he told her, maintaining his hold on her breast until her eyelashes fluttered and her eyes opened wide.

Dylan's breath caught in his throat, captivated by her gaze. For a moment, she simply stared and then confusion and fear set in. Immediately she tried to sit up and cried out when she found herself bound to the bed. She looked down at her nakedness and the hold he had around her breasts. He moved his thumb over the top of the mound to soothe her.

"Relax. You are safe. I will not harm you," he reassured. "I just want to have a talk to you."

"Mark? It looks like you but it doesn't feel like you," she said sleepily. "And you sound British? What's going on? Am I still dreaming?"

Dylan sat on the side of the bed smiling and continuing to fondle and caress her breast, knowing she was still drowsy. She moaned softly, still trying to fully wake herself from the heavy sedation.

"That's because I'm not. I am Mark's identical twin brother, Dylan. Remember?"

"Brother? He never said he had a brother, let alone a twin."

Dylan raised his eyes and shook his head.

"You've already said that. He wouldn't. We don't exactly get on."

He looked down at her nipple, loving the feel of its sudden erectness. He flexed it back and forth, watching the way it moved for a minute.

"Why is that?"

She was breathless. Good. It would make her interrogation a little easier.

He wanted to draw her nipple into his mouth and suckle on it.

"We don't get on. It's a long story. A family thing," he informed her, amused by her questions while bending his lips to the tip until they hovered over the plum teat. He heard her breathe hard as his breath settled over it. He moved closer, consumed with the need to taste her. She pulled on her bonds, arching her body upward as though to thrust her nipple into his mouth.

"You look so alike. I can barely tell you apart."

Dylan's taut, athletic frame tensed automatically. He frowned and lifted his head from her breast, the moment gone.

"We may look the same but I can assure you we are not alike. Our mother could attest to that if she was still alive," he told her with a cutting tone.

"Why do you not get on with Mark?"

"Enough. Have some water. You look parched."

He let go of her breast to pour her a glass of water by the four-post bed draped in white voile curtains tied at each post matching the white silk bedding trimmed with taupe. Glancing at the beautiful crystal chandelier providing the light in the room above the bed in the high ceiling, he couldn't help thinking the room was fit for a Venetian princess. Drew suited it well.

He sat back down on the bed and scooped his hand underneath her head to lift it from the sheets. He put the glass to her lips and bade her to drink. She took several small sips, but he wanted her to drink more and encouraged her to take a long drink before he lowered her back down.

"So who are you and why have you tied me down to this bed? I took you for police or something," she asked cautiously.

"I am of sorts. I am an agent for Interdefense and my name is Dylan Dexter. I want to ask you some questions and I have heard you are a hard woman to pin down," he said with a grin. "So I am not taking any chances; that is why you are tied to the bed until I have all the information I need and I can keep you safe from harm. Have some more water."

He reached for the jug of water again.

"No, no, I already feel uncomfortable and want to relieve myself."

Another grin that made Drew frown. Dylan placed his hand gently over her lower stomach and pressed down.

"Hey, don't do that," Drew implored. "It's uncomfortable. I really need to go to the bathroom."

Dylan pressed down again. "You aren't going anywhere."

"But I don't want to wet myself."

"I don't believe you are in Venice alone. Who are you with?"

"I need to go."

"Focus, Drew. The woman you are with is in just as much

danger as you. You aren't doing her any favors by hiding her. She needs to be picked up. Where is Cally Black?"

The spy increased the pressure of his hand on her stomach. Drew whimpered and squirmed.

"She is here to find answers with me about the disappearance of her daughter. She has been sighted here. We aren't going to trust anyone in authority. The police have obstructed us and done everything they can to stop us from finding her. They are working for James Sumner and your father. I won't tell you where she is. I won't."

"You will."

"No. I can't."

"I think you need a little more water."

Dylan stood up and poured some more water. He lifted her head easily, subduing her resistance when she tried to keep it down on the bed and put the glass to her lips. She clamped them shut but he persisted, pressing the rim of the glass to them hard until she was forced to give in. Quickly he poured the clear liquid into her mouth. She spluttered a little but he was satisfied some of the water had gone down her throat. He lowered her head back down on the bed and replaced his hand over her stomach to exert some pressure. Again she squirmed.

What are you going to do next, waterboard me?" she spat.

"No. I have no need for such crude methods here. I think the threat of losing control and wetting the bed is much more of an incentive for you. Now where is she?"

"You can't do this. She will be in more danger. And every minute you make me lie here, you are putting my daughter in danger. I have to find her."

"We will find your daughter. Where is Cally? I will keep her safe and find her daughter as well. You have my word."

"I can't. I can't trust you."

"You have no choice," he told her firmly, moving his fingers down to slide inside her pussy. Time to step up the pleasure/torture and release her tongue.

She was dry when he first stroked the gentle pink folds, but he persisted and was satisfied when they began to become plump and wet with unexpected arousal. Her hips rose from the bed as his free hand flattened on her lower abdomen. Her bladder would be full to the brim now and the more he aroused her the more she would find it difficult to contain her water. After experiencing the pleasure, he would turn up the heat on the torture until she gave in.

"We know you are investigating the kidnap and trafficking of women from the US and UK into Europe. We also know many of them come through Rome and Venice before being moved onto the Arab states and into Eastern Europe and that you have evidence it is my father organizing the operation."

"Yes. I heard him in conversation with my husband, James

Sumner. I have been following them and gathering evidence. My husband's company is laundering money for the operation. He also arranged for the kidnap of Cally's daughter when your father took a liking to her. She only just turned nineteen and he wants her for himself. He is a monster. No wonder your mother ran from him all those years ago and brought Mark to New York when he was a child."

Dylan closed his eyes, thinking of his father and his disgusting habits and the way he treated women. Nausea rose. He calmed himself and forced himself to concentrate on the matter at hand. Raising his hand from Drew's pussy he brought it down to give it a sharp slap. Her body bucked and rose from the bed in response, prompting him to repeat the action three more times.

"Tell me where she is, Drew. By keeping silent you are going to get her killed."

He whipped her pussy with his hand and was surprised to find his hand striking creamy wetness as he did so. She was a wonderful submissive.

"Please, I can't hold it. Stop," she begged, her chest heaving.

"No. You will hold it or I will take my belt to your bottom. You will hold it as long as you hold out on telling me what I need to know."

He stopped spanking her damp, glistening vagina and returned his attention to her abdomen in the region of her bladder and lowered his hand hard. Drew cried out and strained on her bonds, raising her body from the bed in a futile attempt to struggle free.

"Please, please," she sobbed.

"All you have to do is tell me where she is."

Dylan glanced down at her pussy, waiting for the first drops of water to dribble onto the bed as she lost control. He pressed down even harder.

"She's at a small hotel down one of the back streets. Hotel Cortelli. I can't remember the street."

"We will find it. Hold your water or you will be disciplined. What name is she using?"

"Taylor Wright."

"Good girl. Continue to hold your water."

He removed his hand and took out his mobile from the inside pocket of his suit jacket and called the Italian substation. He spoke fluent Italian. The woman would be picked up immediately. He replaced the phone and looked down at Drew. She was moving agitatedly on the bed trying to curl her legs up to ease the cramping she felt in her stomach. Dylan's cock hardened and twitched with arousal at the sight of her reluctant captivity, wanting to be inside her riding her into submission.

"When are you going to let me go? You can't keep me here tied up on this bed forever."

He leaned over and pinched her nipple, stretching it out idly as he sighed with impatience.

"You will stay here until you realize I am in control and I have your obedience, Drew, and your assurance you will stop investigating and let us deal with the matter alone. My twin would never forgive me if I allowed you to be put in any more danger," he whispered seductively. "He is on his way to Venice and I am sure he will be itching to discipline you over his knee for running from him."

She was tight-lipped. Dylan traced his finger down her stomach and stroked above her pussy, careful not to brush the top of the curls. He watched her chest rise and fall in agitation betraying her arousal at his touch. He couldn't take his eyes from her. To his annoyance she was once more captivating him.

"Please, I need to relieve myself. I am in agony. Untie me," she demanded with a confidence he couldn't help but admire.

Dylan smiled and continued his caress.

"No. You will relieve yourself into a bedpan."

The horror on her face was stark.

"No, no I can't, please," she begged.

Ignoring her pleas, he stood up and reached under the bed. The bedpan was there just where he had instructed it to be left. He brought it out and lifted her legs up before she could complain, forcing her to raise her bottom in the air. Neatly he placed the bedpan underneath her bottom and firmly pressed her hips down when she refused to lower her body onto it.

Cruelly he sat back down on the bed beside her, determined she would learn to respect the power he had over her and pee when commanded.

"Pee and then we will talk some more," he instructed, folding his arms.

"No, no, I can't with you here. What about your assistant? Can't she help me?" Drew was fretful and blushing with embarrassment at the helpless position she found herself in, but he wasn't moving.

"No. Pee."

"I am desperate."

"Do as you are told," he told her calmly. "Learn to obey me."

They sat in silence for a few minutes. Dylan watched her wrestle with her need to relieve herself and her wilful determination to keep control. When she finally decided to give in and sob a little because of it, she found she couldn't actually pee because she was too tense.

"I can't. It won't come," she said through her tears.

Dylan softened his hardened, handsome features and stroked his fingers along the inside of her thigh.

"Let me help you."

"How?"

"Let me touch you. Let me help you cum and your muscles will relax and your water will flow," he told her softly.

"But I can't do that…"

"Yes you can."

Dylan moved his fingers close to her sex this time, allowing his fingers to lightly brush the curls at the side. Her face contorted with pain and she strained upward on her bonds.

"My stomach is cramping so much. I have to pee," she said, distressed. "All right, please help me. Please. I hate you for this."

"Hush. Open your legs as wide as you can get them."

He knew she would find this difficult in the position she had been bound, but he wanted to see her straining to accommodate his request and obey him. She moaned with discomfort as she opened her legs.

"Keep them open," he instructed, knowing it would be a challenge for her.

Using his index finger, he stroked the length of her pussy once more, surprised at the amount of juice dwelling there from her interrogation.

"You are so wet. I think discipline is good for you. It will set boundaries and help you respect my authority over you as well as Mark while we find your daughter. It might stop you putting your life in danger and trying to do all of this alone."

Relishing in being able to caress the woman and gain a point over his brother, Dylan kissed the small bud between her folds with his lips. He heard Drew give a small moan of unexpected pleasure, giving him an immense sense of satisfaction. She tasted sweet. Dylan slipped out his tongue and lightly began to lap at her clit, momentarily taking time to tuck the jewel behind his teeth and suck as though it were a milk teat on her breast. He cupped her buttocks with his hands to lift her up to him.

The more he sucked and tasted, the more he wanted of her. She was fresh, vibrant, and pure in his dark sordid little world of torture, pain, loss, and fury. Dylan's whole frame relaxed as he sank into the welcoming arms of a new addiction—giving pleasure to the captive woman under his protection.

Drew's hips lifted up in response. Involuntarily she pushed her pussy against his open mouth and bucked with each expert stroke of his tongue. Pleased with her response, Dylan circled the tip of his tongue around the soft silky entrance of her channel, building anticipation.

The spy's captive moved her hips restlessly in his grip and he held them tighter to hold her in position. He couldn't help but curl his lips with triumph that the tigress was actually feeling out of control and pleasured by him. It made him step up his game. He nudged the tip of his lithe, slick tongue just inside the small hall and held it there for a moment. There was frustration in her cries this time and wickedly he made her wait knowing the pain of pleasure was fighting with her need to relieve herself. It was a potent aphrodisiac for them both.

With one hard thrust he buried his tongue inside her as far as it would go. Drew's hips lifted up and she furiously bucked against him. The effect of her sexy body demanding more with her hips, straining on her bonds to free herself from the torment just about drove him crazy. He wanted to be inside her.

Her panting grew louder and a rush of silky fluid filled his mouth. Drew was close. Lifting up, he settled her back on the bedpan and quickly replaced his tongue with first one and then two of his fingers, using his thumb to maintain the caress on her clit. He stood and leaned over her, watching her helpless pleasure begin to consume her.

"Cum for me now, Drew, and let your water flow," he breathed his command in a husky voice.

With a cry, Drew let go and allowed her orgasm to blossom. The sight was breathtaking. Her pretty, tense features relaxed and were bathed in a soft pink glow. Her eyes glazed as though she were possessed by pleasure and stared up at him in wonder, making him catch his breath. If he had to say when he first fell in love with Drew Sumner and vowed to steal her from his twin brother, it was this intoxicating moment.

The muscles inside the depths of her vagina tightened and trapped his fingers. He thrusted them harder, deeper as her climax broke, reveling in the feeling of them being inside her connecting them together. The moment she came, her confined water released and flowed freely over his fingers and hand to fall noisily into the pan.

"Good girl," he whispered as her climax ended and the trickle of water into the pan ceased.

Dylan continued moving his fingers back and forth until the small shudders inside her channel relaxed and he made sure every last drop of water had been expelled. Then slowly he removed his fingers and her panting calmed.

Without a word, he walked to the bathroom and retrieved a cleansing wipe with which he lovingly dabbed her vagina to clean her. He returned to dispose of the wipe and took the bedpan away.

Drew grimaced, blushing scarlet. She fought to turn her face and body away from the sight of him taking the pan away.

"Why does this bother you? It should not. I nursed my bedridden grandfather who raised me before he died," he said, giving a small chuckle. "And believe me, this is not the first time I have made a woman urinate when cumming," he said, brushing his fingers over her thigh and feeling the urge to continue the small cruelty of talking about her perceived shame.

"There is nothing more intoxicating than taking control of a woman's pleasure and the function of her body in doing so. In that moment she is completely in your control, dependent on you to take care of her." He lowered his voice to a soft whisper. "Complete trust must exist. I hope in time this is something we can cultivate between us."

"I am not sure I can ever trust a man who has kidnapped me and is holding me here against my will," she answered defiantly.

He smiled and continued to caress the inside of her thigh amused and undeterred, the predator inside him curling his lip with the thrill of the challenge to bring her to her knees in front of him.

"We will see."

He washed his hands, his mind excitedly dwelling on the seductive image of her cumming as he conquered her will. The thought of curling up in bed with her and holding her softness against him was too tempting. It was a challenge he was determined to meet. Drew was willingly going to be his, and this time his brother was going to lose the fight.

9

Dylan sat at the back of the water taxi with Drew a couple of hours later. He'd made sure she had eaten and been given the once-over by the doctor before allowing her out. It was a risk he didn't want to take, but he needed her to question Sumner's Aunt Alessandra regarding Eva's whereabouts.

He frowned, watching her rub her stomach.

"Are your injuries still stinging?"

"No. The pain relief the doctor gave me is working well. This is period pain. Nothing more," she confessed, looking back out at the tourists walking over the bridge in front of them just before they passed underneath it.

He smiled to himself. She could barely make eye contact with him even now after her interrogation. It was only a matter of hours before Mark arrived to reclaim her, and he was going to have to move fast if he wanted to steal the prize out from under him.

The water taxi neared its mooring outside the small palazzo that Sumner had bought for his aunt, a native to Venice, nine years ago.

"Stay by my side and do everything I tell you," Dylan told her, taking out his weapon from its holster around his chest to check before replacing it. The aunt had protection and he wanted to make sure he was ready so he could fiercely protect Drew at a moment's notice if the situation became difficult.

She nodded as he climbed out of the boat and turned to offer his hand to help her out. She took it gratefully even though she still couldn't meet his eyes and climbed out. Instructing the water taxi to stay put, he walked up to the door of the palazzo in a long canal street not far from the Grand Canal.

A maid answered the door.

"Yes, can I help you?" she asked in Italian.

"Yes, we have come to see Signora Cavalli."

"I am sorry, Sir. She is not here."

The maid looked nervous and started to close the door on them. Dylan shot out his hand and pushed it hard, forcing the maid to back away into the lobby. Taking Drew's arm, he guided her into the building and slammed the door closed behind them.

"Where is your mistress?" Dylan demanded in English.

"I told you, Sir, she is not here."

"You are lying. Where is she hiding the girl?"

The young maid backed away.

"I don't know what you are talking about. Please leave."

"No. Where is the girl?"

"Marcello, Marcello!" the maid screamed for help as Dylan took hold of her arm.

A stocky man in his fifties came out of one of the rooms and lunged at Dylan, who reacted quickly, pushing Drew to one side and tackling his attacker. A quick turn with a roundhouse kick to his stomach had the man falling backward onto the tiled floor. Dylan was standing over him before he could rise, pulling him up to deliver a hard punch to his face and another to his stomach before executing another kick that sent him to the floor. He slid along the floor with force to crash his head into the marble and gilt table leg, which dazed him before he fell unconscious.

"Drew, find something to tie him up with," Dylan ordered, taking hold of the maid's arm again. He put his hand around her throat in a careful but firm hold and pulled her back against him in one sharp movement.

Drew stared at him wide-eyed, shocked with what she had just witnessed.

"Now, Drew, before he wakes up," the spy shouted, making the maid walk forward to the wall.

He pushed her up against it and tightened the grip on her throat.

"Hands behind your back," he instructed.

"Please don't hurt me," the maid begged, doing as she was told.

"Tell me where Alessandra has gone."

"I can't tell you. I don't know."

Dylan groaned. For the second time that day he was going to have to force information from a woman. Why did they not realize he always won and just give in?

He wove his arm underneath hers and noticed that Drew was finishing tying the man to the table leg by his wrists with some ribbons she'd found keeping together an arrangement of flowers together in a large tall vase on top of the table in front of a long thin mirror. Dylan shook his head. It wouldn't hold and would probably snap. He had to move fast to get the information out of the girl before the big guy woke up.

"Drew, over here now."

Dylan moved the girl to another table, one that was oval and in the middle of the room with a large fern on top of it underneath the red tulip-shaped Murano glass chandelier hanging above it on the fresco ceiling covered in cherubs and beautiful goddesses in a garden setting.

"Take the fern off the table."

Drew did as she was bid and stood holding the plant, watching as Dylan placed the girl over the table face-down and held her there by the arms, holding the side of her face down onto the cool white marble surface.

"I will make you tell me," he hissed at the maid.

"Drew, lift up her skirt and pull down her panties."

"What?"

"Do it now or when we get out of this you will be over my knee for the spanking of your life. Now."

Drew jumped to attention. Putting the plant down, she tentatively moved toward the girl.

"Hurry up. We haven't got much time."

Drew closed her eyes and then sighed. She set her face straight and reached in between Dylan and the maid to force her tight pencil skirt up her legs, then thighs, and over her suspenders holding up a pair of nude stockings. Dylan raised his eyebrows and watched with some amusement and interest at the way she gently slid her soft slender hands over the girl's pale thighs to tuck her fingers around the top of the material of her panties and slowly pull them down until the girl's pale bottom was bared.

"Hold her arms until I take off my belt."

"What are you going to do?" the maid demanded in a panicked voice.

"Thrash it out of you," he said, pulling hard on her arms before letting go and raising her from the table until she hovered above it in an uncomfortable position.

"By the time I finish with whipping your backside you won't be able to sit down for a week. So anytime you feel like telling me, let me know and the pain will stop," he snarled in her ear. But all he got in return was whimpering. Forcefully he placed her back down on the table and motioned for Drew to take over.

Dylan stepped back and undid his silver belt buckle that matched his cufflinks, glancing at the man who was moaning and coming back around. He approached the girl but then stopped, surprised.

Drew was pushing the girl down on the table and shouting at her.

"Where did that bitch take my daughter?"

She raised her slender hand and slapped one of the girl's buttocks. It was an admirable strike with some power behind it, but it only produced some small cries from the girl. It needed a firm male palm to induce some stinging pain to get the girl to think and reconsider her decision not to be cooperative.

Drew was trying to put more power behind her slaps, catching the backs of the girl's thighs when he approached.

"Hold her face down on the table."

Drew nodded and moved to execute his order with speed.

"You are getting the hang of this," he grinned, taking hold of the maid's arms and forcing them to remain backward and lift upward into the air to cause her discomfort. Twisting to the side, he raised the belt and struck the maid's bottom hard with it.

The belt thwacked at one buttock then the next, with the speed each time increasing the intensity of each lash. The girl screamed out, her flesh wobbling and jumping with every strike coloring a nice hot pink.

"Please stop," she begged when he was in mid-swing.

"Are you ready to talk?"

Silence.

This time the spy aimed the belt at the backs of her thighs with an expert stroke, watching it snap at her tender skin and leaving its mark.

"Stop. She has taken the child to Roma to meet her father. That is all I know. I heard them say they were going to take her away and hide her with another family and change her name."

"A maid that eavesdrops. What fantastic luck," Dylan mocked.

"Do you know the name of the family? It began with a D—Day, De, or something."

Dylan lowered the belt and glanced at Drew. Expectancy hung in the air.

"Dexter?" he questioned.

"Yes. I am sure it was them."

Drew stood up and put her hands to her face in shock and horror as Dylan covered his mouth and smoothed it over the neatly groomed facial hair around his mouth fashioned in exactly the same way as his twin. Sumner was a bastard giving his child to Lewis Dexter. The man wasn't fit to keep a dog, let alone a child. She would be abused. The aunt must not know about the Dexter family's history. Both he and Mark had been beaten by the man as children along with their mother. From the information he had been given on Alessandra she doted on the child and wouldn't let go of her so easily, especially if she knew what his father and stepmother were really like. Maybe the plan was for her to live with them and stay with the child—something the Dexters would no doubt remedy in time with her death if necessary.

He quickly replaced his belt, noticing the big guy in the corner was fully awake and pulling at his bonds, shouting at them full-tilt. Dylan caught hold of Drew and propelled her toward the door and back out to the water taxi.

Dylan watched Drew with concern. Tears had formed in her eyes and she was doing her damned hardest not to shed them. She looked afraid and exhausted. The driver was staring at her, and she looked like she needed some privacy. He took hold of her arm and guided her straight into the covered part of the water taxi to talk to her. The moment he closed the door behind them she burst into tears and sank down on the long blue leather seat. She put her face in her hands. Dylan sat next to her.

"I can't believe James would do that. Our little girl. How could he hurt her and deprive her of my love? She needs her mother and I need her. I've let her down. I've lost her. What if they have hurt her? Oh, my God what am I going to do? I did this to her."

Dylan shook his head at her and without hesitating put his arms around her, drawing her against his chest. He held her heaving body tight against his frame and kissed the top of her head while his hand moved soothingly up and down her arm.

"Shh. We will get Eva back. Placing Eva with my father will force you to go back to James, but it looks like my father has lost patience and just wants to kill you. His new younger wife wants a child. She can't carry any full term. This will be my father's way of giving her what she wants. I won't rest until we get Eva back," he reassured her, kissing the top of her head. He reached down to tuck his fingers underneath her chin and lifted her face up to his. He looked directly into her eyes, loving the light dusting of freckles across her nose and the tops of her cheeks. "I promise I will find her and bring her back to you."

She stared up at him like a child and every instinct in him yearned to protect her. He'd never felt anything so strong in his life for a woman before. It was almost overpowering. Without warning he found himself lowering his lips to brush them against hers. She did not object and obediently parted her lips as he sought to deepen the kiss. Clasping the back of her head to hold her steady in place, he quickly dominated her mouth, taking firm control of the kiss. He was beginning to intensify the kiss, loving the way she purred with satisfaction against him, when suddenly the driver opened the door from his standing position at the wheel and shouted down to him, ruining the moment.

"I need you up here. Another taxi is coming toward us and I don't like the look of the people on it. I don't know them and there aren't many people driving taxis in Venezia that I do not know. I think they have guns. There is another one behind us."

"Stay here," Dylan instructed, getting to his feet. "Get on the floor and keep your head down," he said, helping her down. She gave him a fearful look. He grinned and kissed the top of her head.

"Relax, I know what I am doing. I will keep you safe so you can look after that daughter of yours."

Dylan made his way out of the cabin. The bearded driver gestured with his eyes to the front of the water taxi.

"They've come to get the girl."

Dylan frowned, noticing a boat slowly coming toward them behind two gondolas. There were three men on board and no passengers. The canal was barely wide enough for them to pass and it would be easy for them to jump onboard and kill Drew. To get a better look at the threat from behind, the agent leaned over the side of the boat. The second motorboat taxi also contained three men and no passengers. Like the men in front they appeared armed. The only thing keeping them from getting close was the slow movement they were forced to maintain because of the gondolas littering the long thin narrow canal behind and in front of them.

A wave of claustrophobia washed over Dylan. He hated feeling trapped. Time to get out of this damn tunnel. He looked to his left as the driver eyed him cautiously waiting for an instruction. An escape route was presenting itself.

"What do you want me to do?" the driver asked desperately.

Dylan didn't speak as the turning came up. He simply took hold of the steering wheel with one hand and rotated it left in a sharp motion, forcing the boat to turn. The driver growled and cursed as the water taxi's back end slid wide outward, nearly hitting the wall of the building on the right to complete the maneuver. The boat rocked violently, making them both have to fight to keep their balance standing up.

The canal they now found themselves in was clear of gondolas and other boats, a back street. Dylan took out his weapon and moved to the side of the boat, glancing back.

"Put your foot down and get us out of here."

The driver nodded and the speed of the boat increased. Dylan wanted it to go faster but he knew it was too dangerous around the crumbling brick walls of the sinking damp buildings hemming them in. Ignoring his claustrophobia, he looked over the side again. Sure enough, the boats were now turning down the street after them and continuing the pursuit, matching their speed.

"How long until we get out of this maze?" Dylan demanded.

"At the bottom of here we can turn down to the Bridge of Sighs and then out to the Grand Canal."

"That's when they will really come after us. We need to be prepared."

"Just get us out of here and back to the safe house on Branzillo Island."

Dylan turned back to the cabin and walked through it to get to the back of the boat. He glanced down at Drew and paused briefly to rest his hand on her shoulder.

Dylan continued moving, but the sound of a shot and a bullet piercing one of the panes of glass in the wooden doors leading to the back of the boat made them all jump with surprise. The glass shattered and sprayed across the cabin as the bullet traveled through it and penetrated the leather seat cover.

"Keep your head down, Drew, and don't move."

As another bullet hit the side of the boat, Dylan made his way through what was left of the wooden, glass-paned doors at the back to face the men pursuing them.

They were closer now and the men on both boats were shooting at them full-tilt, forcing Dylan to return fire. The boat on the left revved its engine hard and came closer. One of the men crawled onto the bow of the boat and crouched precariously on top of it, ready to jump and board the water taxi.

Dylan bent down trying to avoid being shot by one of the men on the second boat, his eyes flicking constantly to the other man ready to jump onto the water taxi. There was too much fire coming from the second boat for him to turn his attention to the man. He was going to come aboard and there was nothing the Englishman could do to stop him at that moment. Luckily there was another turn coming up.

There was a loud thud and the boat rocked from side to side. The man was in the boat. He ignored Dylan and made straight for the cabin. Dylan had to risk it. He fired another shot and turned to tackle the assailant. He caught him from behind and spun him around to face fire from the second boat using him as a human shield. A shot rang out and traveled underneath a small overhead bridge to slice into the man's chest. A second wounded his leg when Dylan forced the killer's body to twist and shield him once more. The man jumped and shook against Dylan before collapsing.

No longer viable as a shield and with another man trying to jump into the boat, Dylan dragged the assailant to the side of the boat and pushed him into the canal, ducking to avoid another low bridge overhead. He fell in the path of the second boat and was hit head-on as it came close to allow another man to board.

The objective in Dylan's mind was clear: Protect the journalist at all costs even if it meant the loss of his own life and others. It was his purpose. Years in the SAS and then MI5 had taught him it well. Now working for Interdefense with the safety of Europe and the world at risk in an age filled with terrorists and unknown enemies, he felt it more keenly. He was born to be a soldier and a protector. It was in his DNA and if it meant being mercenary in a dangerous world, then so be it. His moral code would allow it without any guilt.

The dead man in the water slowed down the second boat but another assailant was already jumping into the back of the water taxi from the first just as the boat lurched to the side to make the turn into the Rio di Palazzo containing the Bridge of Sighs. Dylan tackled the man the moment he landed in the boat, but this one wasn't going to lie down easy.

He took a punch to his jaw that knocked the sunglasses from his face, but dropping the Glock he quickly blocked a second. The water taxi gathered more momentum and raced toward the Grand Canal, narrowly avoiding other taxis and gondolas by weaving in and out of them. One of the gondoliers shook his fist at the boat as it created a backwash that nearly sent him and his two lovebird passengers tumbling into the canal.

Dylan grabbed hold of the man's arm and twisted his leg around the assailant's. He made the move fast and it brought the killer down hard on the deck of the boat. The agent turned the man's outstretched arm behind his back hard until it snapped. To dispose of him he pushed him to the side ready to knock him from the water taxi as it made a good distance from the other two boats. It sped under the cold grey Bridge of Sighs, which was aptly named because it was the bridge on which criminals crossed to the prison and received their last glimpse of Venice. The legend said they sighed as they did so.

But the assailant fought back, managing to twist his broken arm out of the spy's grip. He aimed his weapon clumsily in his left hand. Dylan tightened his jaw and banged his forearm against the man's with force. It flew out of his hand across the small deck at the back of the boat. Dylan punched him in the face hard as he tried to reach for the weapon again. He kept hitting the attacker, pushing him backward to the side of the boat.

Unable to take any more, the assailant slumped to his knees, blood pouring from his nose. Dylan pulled him up by the lapels of his leather jacket and sat his limp, dazed body on the brass side rail as the taxi traveled under a large bridge marking the entrance into the Grand Canal. People standing on the steps of the bridge taking photos of the Bridge of Sighs were shouting and pointing looking down at them as Dylan took hold of the man's legs and lifted him up and backward over the side making the boats chasing them that had gained ground swerve to avoid him. The splash echoed around the walls of the bridge before the water taxi broke free into the wide expanse of the Grand Canal and out toward the islands.

The motorboats following them maintained their pursuit, making Dylan duck when another bullet bounced off the polished raised wood in the back of the boat. He picked up the assailant's weapon and stood to return fire when the wailing of police sirens made him pause. Two police boats moved in behind the water taxi, forcing the other two boats to slow and stop shooting.

Dylan grinned at them as they looked on with frustration while the water taxi escaped. The police boats had been sent by command to help after the driver had called them. He lowered the inferior weapon the killer had used and retrieved his Glock from the floor, replacing it into his suit jacket. He picked up his designer sunglasses and put them back on. He fastened his suit jacket, smoothing it down to correct his slightly disheveled appearance, happy with the outcome. He returned to Drew to make sure she was all right.

10

Drew was quiet when they reached the island. As he helped her step from the boat she put her hand to her head and slumped. She gasped, afraid she was going to hit the floor of the wooden jetty, but Dylan scooped her up into his arms before she knew what was happening and carried her up to the large palazzo with ease. She rested her head on his chest, prompting him to hold her tighter and make her feel safe.

He had a conference with the agents under him and requested the police in Rome to hunt down Alessandra before she connected with his father. A while later Dylan found Drew curled up on a chaise lounge in one her rooms watching Italian TV. She'd been told to rest and stay in bed by the doctor, but clearly she wasn't in the mood for listening. She stared motionless at the screen with her beautiful sea-blue eyes filled with tears obviously unable to understand what the actors were saying to each other in the soap opera because unlike him she didn't speak Italian. He frowned, noticing she was rubbing her tummy again.

Instead of remonstrating her and carrying her back to the bedroom he decided to see if there was anything he could do to at least take the pain away in her stomach. He wished he could get her child back and carry Eva in his arms to give to her right now. But it was a waiting game. For the first time in years his heart ached for someone else. He'd never allowed anyone to get that close. Not after it broke when his mother left to run away from his cruel violent father with Mark for New York and never came back, leaving him stranded with his father. It was a strange feeling to have again.

He bent in front of Drew and cupped her face with his hand tilting it up toward him. His thumb stroked her cheek lovingly. They hadn't spoken about their kiss in the water taxi.

"What is wrong? Why are you in pain? And don't fob me off. I want to know how to help you. Is it period pain?"

She looked squarely into his eyes when she spoke. "None of your business. I can handle it. Now let me go."

He winced inwardly, her tone spearing him.

"No, I won't. I will get you some painkillers," he snapped.

"No. I won't take them."

"Then I will make you."

"Try it," she challenged.

Her anger had built. He got it. She felt useless sitting there while her child was missing. Dylan was about to retaliate when she let out a cry and bent over nursing her stomach again. He couldn't help but rub her back.

"Don't touch me," she screamed, standing to get away from

him. Her reaction made him pull away and pace as she knelt on the floor and rocked her body in an attempt to soothe the pain. He couldn't bear to see her suffering. He decided to take action and pulled her up from the polished wood floor. Drew struggled like a wildcat and he had to use all of his male strength to hold her and drag her to the sofa.

The spy sat down at one end of the sofa and stretched his long legs out along its length hauling her body on top of his. To cease her struggles, he closed his hand around her throat in a careful hold, pressing a little tighter to make her stop moving. Drew's hands gripped his arm trying to remove his hand. It was futile. Holding her in place, Dylan pulled her red skirt up her legs ripping the material as he did so. He quickly thrust his hand down inside her panties to reach her pussy.

"If you won't take any medication then I will give you some of my own homespun medicine, a good orgasm," he said. There was a snippet of humor in his voice. "That always makes the blood flow and stops the pain. I am guessing you aren't on yet. Trust me, this will help. Now stop struggling, lie back, and relax."

Dylan pinched her clit to encourage some good behavior.

"Stop moving your legs and relax. I won't hurt you. You enjoyed me touching you the last time. Learn to trust me."

"You were interrogating me," she screamed.

"You still enjoyed it," he teased.

Softly, gently, Dylan began to caress the full swollen lips of her sex confined in her panties that he kept in place to catch the first drops of her menstrual blood. He kept his hand around her throat and looked down at her lovingly when she gave him a delicate moan. Satisfied she was warming to the idea and inviting him to continue, he circled one of his fingers around her entrance, preparing to penetrate her with it. Now he felt her hips buck upward and the first flush of wetness coat her vagina to ease his path inside her.

Soaking his finger, he eased it up inside her using the pad of his thumb to caress her clit and her flooding lips. He heard her pant as he pushed his finger deeper. More moans of pleasure forced themselves from her mouth and he became satisfied when her hips pushed her body down onto his finger trying to catch more of it up inside. He joined the first finger with a second and reached higher, stroking the velvet wet walls rhythmically before curling it to make contact with the rough back wall of her vagina, the G-spot.

At this point Drew's hips rose into the air and her passionate cries became helpless, wanton, and abandoned. The sound enthralled him. The agent felt his need to dominate her surge and triumph in his control of her body. He intensified his stroking action, watching her face flush with a warm rosy glow. His thumb caressed the softness of her neck as he continued to hold her fragile throat to keep her in check and at his command. He kissed the side of her cheek.

"Good girl. Let me take you there and remove some of this nasty pain," he breathed, feeling his cock tensing and rising up toward her bottom moving with the rhythm set by her hips.

She was close.

"Come for me, Drew. Surrender," he whispered seductively in her ear.

A small cry rang out from her lips and she was climaxing strongly. She panted and bucked like a bitch in heat. Dylan pressed his thumb down hard on the middle of her vagina between the lips as she started to ride, her pleasure increasing the sensitivity of the experience.

"What are you doing to me?" she said breathless. "It's too strong. I…I can't," was all she could say as the first wave of pleasure knocked her sideways. Then she was sobbing, her intense relief lost in deep ecstasy.

Eventually she calmed and rested back against his chest, recovering her normal breathing pattern. Dylan watched her brushing his lips across her cheek once more.

He loosened his hold on her throat and she was quick to take advantage, standing up to remove his fingers still gently caressing her pussy. He stood next to her as she pulled down her ripped skirt. He glanced at his finger. There was a small amount of scarlet menstrual blood on it, but less than he'd hoped for. He rubbed it with his thumb, watching her cheeks warm with embarrassment at his action. With a grin that he knew would only serve to infuriate her, he walked to the table to pick up a tissue. He liked her angry with him, he decided. She set his blood thumping and kept him on his toes despite his annoyance. He liked the game but eventually she would realize she had no hope of winning it. He was going to be the master in this relationship and all of her pretense and denial she didn't want it that way would come to an end soon. But for now he was content to indulge her fantasy, lulling her into a false sense of security before he pounced and claimed her from his brother.

Dylan rubbed his hand gently along her stomach after cleaning the small droplet of blood from his finger with the tissue.

"That should get everything flowing eventually and make the pain a lot easier," he told her softly as he stood up from the sofa.

He walked to the bathroom and found a box of tampons. The Interdefense team had made sure all of her needs were catered for. When he returned to the room with them she reached to take them from him. The spy pulled them back and with a wide smile wagged his finger at her.

"No, I will insert it."

"Don't be ridiculous," Drew stammered.

Her blushing features made him want to laugh and soothe her all at the same time. His lips began to curl into a smile once more, but when her eyes darkened he softened it.

"I will care for you. From now on when you need to change the tampon you will come to me." He made sure his tone was calm but firm.

Perhaps this control over the function of her menstrual cycle would convince her of his mastery and his protection.

"No, I won't. You can't expect me to take you seriously."

It wasn't a question, more of a statement.

"Then you will be spanked and confined to bed until you capitulate to my demands. As your protector and bodyguard you are under my care and I will tend to all of your needs."

"You wouldn't dare."

He chuckled.

"Drew, you should know by now I am a man who always carries out his threats. Raise your skirt and open your legs now or I will do it for you."

Drew turned to walk away, displaying a look of contempt. He caught her arm in a rough grip and brought her back close to his chest.

"Don't walk away from me. I won't stand for it. My word is law and you will learn to obey me."

"Never."

"Then I will have to make you."

"You keep saying that! Ruthless bastard," she cursed, raising her hand to slap him.

Dylan was quick to grab her hand and force it behind her back. It was quickly joined by the other and before she knew it he was propelling her backward against the wall. Roughly, without mercy, he held her wrists behind her with one strong hand and raised her skirt. Dylan dipped his hands down the front of the skimpy white lace panties once more. He tugged them down, noticing another small droplet of blood staining the gusset and yanked them down to her knees. The agent stood and cupped his hand over her still glistening pussy and he slapped it hard, staring into her eyes.

Drew's body bucked wildly against his hand as he aimed the second blow, which was a little harder than the last and made her gasp out loud. A wild look shone out from those soft eyes tempting him to strike her again to win the war of dominance being played out between them. She wanted him and there was no doubt. He continued delivering the pussy slap with expertise, listening to her defiant cries blossom into delicate gratifying moans.

Dylan hardened, watching her breathlessly bite her swollen pink bottom lip and moan even though she continued to struggle. He had to fight to keep her still, slamming her back against the wall to strike her again. Her resistance made the game between them even more enticing. Never had he wanted to win a battle more. Drew Sumner would submit to him whether self-control allowed it or not. It was just a matter of time before she knelt at his feet and begged him to collar and leash her as his own.

He intensified the slaps, delivering them at high pace, feeling her wetness increase tenfold to soak his palm, making him wonder whether he should take her. She was daring him. The urge was strong and potent. But if he confessed his need she would win the game and he would be at her mercy, under her control. Never would he give himself so freely to a woman.

Besides he was more than sure she would refuse him and his command over her would be lost. He tightened his frame, determined to keep control. Drew was going to be his downfall if he didn't tame his own desire for her.

Dylan moved in close for the last wet strike of her pussy. His desire was ready to burst when his thigh and cock sheathed in his trousers accidentally brushed her own soft bare inner thigh and the gentle dark curl of her sex. It made him grunt. A look of surprised triumph pierced her eyes. Narrowing his own eyes, he immediately ceased the pussy slap to rip her panties down and off her. Letting go of her wrists, he curved his hands around her bottom to hold and squeeze her buttocks. In one sweeping motion, he lifted her up around him. Electricity jolted through him when his clothed cock thrusted against her wet pussy so much that he didn't see the slap across his face coming.

The blow was sharp and it stung, but it only seemed to fire his need for her. It was with practiced self-control that he didn't pull down his zipper and thrust hard inside her. Her little game was now on dangerous ground. If she baited him any further he was going to give her exactly what she truly wanted from him.

With an animalistic noise, he carried her to the table. Bending with her legs locked around his waist he swept everything off the surface, including the vase of flowers. The crystal vase smashed to the floor, scattering starburst lilies and water everywhere. He didn't care. He lay Drew down on the table and gripped her throat with his hand. She panted and looked up at him as he roughly forced her legs apart. He reached for the tampon at the top of the table and with his teeth opened the wrapper. Dylan intensified the grip on her throat, forcing her head up and back and with a careful, gentle, and correctly aimed slap he tapped the side of her face in one quick motion with his hand. She gasped with a sound that was more aroused than shocked. Clearly she liked to be roughly handled.

"Don't move or I will put you to bed naked with your legs raised and open so I can change your tampon when needed.

Do I make myself clear?"

He took her silence to mean he had been understood and let go of her throat to turn his attention to her vagina. She was flooded but there was no more blood when he examined it with his finger. It appeared Drew would be enduring some more PMT anger symptoms before the night was out. A part of him relished the thought of another rough tussle that this time would perhaps end in her begging him to take her. The spy gave Drew's vagina a gentle stroke to soothe her, impressed she was now lying still and breathing hard.

It was by no means the first time he had inserted a tampon into a woman and he knew exactly what to do. Using his fingers, he opened the entrance to her sex nice and wide and slowly fed the tampon up inside her. Content it was comfortably lodged inside her vagina and she was adequately plugged, he closed her legs and lifted her by the arms to sit her on the table. She couldn't look him in the eye and she was blushing like a schoolgirl.

"Good girl. That wasn't too bad, now was it? You made a fuss for nothing."

She glared at his condescending tone, making him smile with satisfaction.

"I will change you in a couple of hours. If I find you have taken it out and changed yourself, I will take my belt to your bottom. Am I understood, Drew?"

She ignored him and started to get up off the table to look across the floor for her panties. He stopped her, gripping her wrists again.

"Answer me, Drew."

"Yes," she hissed.

"Good. Stay where you are."

Dylan let go of her wrists and retrieved her panties.

"They are stained with blood. I will fetch you some fresh ones," he told her, tossing them into the bin.

He smoothed her ripped skirt down, a wave of protectiveness sweeping unexpectedly over him. He liked caring for her. It appeared to come easy to him even though it was a strange feeling. Women were usually just a quick fuck for him. Drew Sumner had his emotions all over the place and whether he liked it or not he was under her spell.

"I want you to get some rest in bed before dinner. Mark will be arriving soon. You look tired. Are you sure I can't get you any medication? A hot water bottle?"

"No, nothing. Thank you. The pain has eased for the moment."

Dylan helped her off the table, making sure she didn't step down into the water to ruin her red suede shoes that made her look so sexy.

"I will get this cleared up," he said, leading her to the bedroom with his palm in the middle of her back. He went straight to her underwear drawer and selected another pair of silk panties the team had provided. He opened them and bent in front of her.

"Lift your skirt and put your feet in."

Blushing again she quietly did as she was told and allowed him to slide the panties up her thighs and smooth the material over the curve of her bottom. When he finished he gently patted one buttock. He led her to the bed and waited until she lay down on top of it.

He leaned over her, noticing those tears gathering again. He caressed her shoulder.

"I let Eva down. I've lost her," she whispered. The tears began to roll down her cheeks. Instinctively he reached to brush them away.

"No, you haven't. I made a promise to you and I intend to keep it. I will bring Eva back to you," he told her with conviction. "Now try to sleep. I will stay with you."

She nodded and smiled, allowing him to stroke her cheek.

"Thank you."

Dylan covered her with a light summer blanket laid across the bottom of the bed and pulled a gray padded armchair to the side of the bed. He sat down on it to guard her.

11

He didn't know what woke him in the chair. Perhaps it was her heels on the wooden floor in the lounge. He wasn't sure. Instantly on alert he opened his eyes wide and looked at the bed. She wasn't in it.

Dylan was on his feet and moving out of the room at speed to stop her walking out the door with a small suitcase in her hand. He caught hold of her arm and swung her back into the room. With the tap of his foot he forced the door to slam shut. His hand wound around her throat, the other around her waist, and he pulled her back against him. She dropped the suitcase and gasped.

"Where the hell do you think you are going?" he shouted. "As if you could even get past the guards outside."

"I need to find Eva. I can't just sit here doing nothing. Damn it. Why are you trying to stop me all of the time?" She finished her sentence with a frustrated scream and began to struggle in his arms like a mad woman to free herself from his stronghold.

"Because it is too dangerous and you will get yourself killed. You won't be any good to Eva when she comes back then, will you?" he shouted in her ear, determined to make her see sense. But she wasn't going to.

Her black heel kicked back against his leg hard again and again, making him decide to take rough action. Holding her throat, he lifted her up against him and carried her to the bedroom. When he reached the bed still keeping the grip on her throat to remind her of his power over her, he propelled her sideways onto it and held her there. She continued to struggle, but the way her eyes looked up at him told him their game of seduction was back on. For a second she stopped struggling and panted. There it was again—that look that told him she wanted to be conquered. He prided himself on knowing enough about women to know when they meant something, but Drew was unpredictable, feisty, and could suddenly surprise him. That was what made her so exciting. He decided to go for it but to exercise caution. If she changed her mind he would back off but for now, game on.

His free hand took hold of the pink flimsy summer dress at the top of the bodice and using all of his potent male strength, he ripped it downward while she continued to squirm and struggle. The shocked cry emanating from her lips was tinged with something else—submissive arousal. He tore the garment from her body.

"When I give you an order I expect you to obey me instantly and to the letter. I am in charge here. Not you," he said, throwing the dress onto the floor after yanking it out from underneath her body. "I am responsible for your protection. I told you to rest and stay in bed. Now I will make you."

He wasted no more time and pulled the flimsy pink thong down her legs and off her feet, throwing her shoes off in the process. Glancing at her pussy with need, he turned her over to face down on the bed so fast that she cried out. All she wore was a pretty pink lace bra. He undid the catch and pulled it down her arms and out from under her.

Gripping her red-gold mane tied up in a bun he pushed her face-down onto the bed and gave her rump two hard slaps. She yelped into the sheets. Re-establishing his hold on her throat, he moved her back across the bed to the side, tugging hard on her hair.

He positioned Drew face-down on the bed with her beautiful big breasts and erect tips squashed into the covers and made her place her feet flat on the floor and bend her knees to keep her still. It was an uncomfortable position and concentrating on maintaining it would tame her anger.

"Open your legs wide." He issued the command with the firm slap of his hand against her bare bottom, giving her a second for good measure. Drew thrust her bottom out at him, jerking with each strike as she moved her legs further apart. With a grin of triumph, he spanked her twice more.

"Good, little one," he said, harshly thrusting his finger between her thighs to locate the tail end of the tampon. With one quick pull it was out and in his hands. He examined it for signs of blood but there was only a fraction. A good deep fucking was going to cure Drew of her PMT, he mused, tossing the tampon away into the bin by the nightstand to deal with later.

A caress of her pussy found it wet. Dylan raised one eyebrow, both amused and taken that she was clearly enjoying his robust behavior with her. His cock tensed with painful need. He had to be inside her before Mark arrived. This was his chance.

He pulled down his zipper. Drew gave a loud cry of delight at hearing the noise.

"Thrust your bottom out at me," he instructed, giving her backside another sharp spank to encourage her obedience before guiding his cock to her soaking wet entrance. There was no time to undress. He would burst if he didn't ride her now.

Squatting his powerfully lean, muscled frame, Dylan tightened the grip on her head, forcing it upward and with one deep pump of his penis he fed himself inside her to the hilt. The low guttural groan she gave told him his dominating presence inside her pussy was more than welcoming. It was as if he was conquering some painful need. His hand curled around her throat once more. He rammed inside her fast and hard, making sure every stroke went deep. She panted and moaned pushing back on him, digging her fingers into the sheets to gather them up and hold on.

He fucked her like a man possessed, loving the feel of her silky wet muscles as his cock caressed her core. He could hear by her tight breathing that she was as close to cumming as he was. He'd wanted to play with her longer but this wasn't the time. He had to stake his claim on her and break her into submission.

"Wait until I give you permission to cum, Drew," he reprimanded, slowing his thrusts right down. It drove Drew wild.

He kept them both close for a while longer, enjoying the control and teasing stroke of his cock inside her and then increased the tempo so hard her body jolted on the bed.

"Cum now, Drew," he ordered, strengthening his grip on her throat. With an animalistic grunt she came and he with her. He roared his release, feeling his seed spurt in a thick torrent along her channel. Finally, the spiral of tormenting pleasure dropped and they both collapsed on the bed.

12

Drew woke to find herself curled up in the sheets of the bed alone. Where had Dylan gone? He'd cradled her in his arms until she'd fallen asleep after their lovemaking and now he was nowhere to be seen. She could hear raised voices. Then she heard a different noise. A loud crash. Then something else smashed outside the bedroom in the lounge area, making her fear that the men chasing her had somehow gotten into the Interdefense Safe House. Wrapping the silk white sheet around her body she smoothed down her hair and rushed through the door. What she saw made her put her hand to her mouth in shock.

Mark and Dylan were fighting. At first all she could do was stare at the stark resemblance between them as identical twins. For a while she couldn't tell them apart. They were both devastatingly handsome, dark-haired, eyes black, smooth complexion apart from the neatly groomed facial hair around their mouths and jawline. Even what they wore was the same. She wanted to laugh. She finally realized who was who when Dylan gave Mark his trademark roundhouse kick to the stomach and sent him sprawling over the chaise longue she'd been lying on earlier, knocking it over. The place was wrecked. Smashed vases lay on the floor. The sofa was overturned and one of the windows looking out over the gardens was broken. She was amazed she'd slept through most of it. Mark got up behind the fallen chaise lounge.

"You couldn't keep your hands off her, could you? You had to steal her from me? Always trying to get me back. Always trying to get one over on me."

Dylan shook his head and wiped a small amount of blood from his lip.

"Just like you stole our mother?"

"What? It always comes back to this, doesn't it?"

They hadn't even noticed she was standing there. Drew was on the verge of interrupting and making her presence known, but the interesting twist in their argument stopped her. Finally, she was about to know more of the saga of Mark's past he'd kept secret from her.

"For the hundredth fucking time. My mother told me she had to get out of the house in a hurry. Our father was trying to kill her. We were eight. She searched for you everywhere, dragging me with her and couldn't find you. She was frantic. She was bleeding after he'd raped and stabbed her. She'd hit him over the head with a frying pan and he was out cold. She had little time. We had to leave you."

"I was just playing in the damn garden with a couple of friends."

"Remember how large the estate was? You could have been anywhere. I hated her for leaving you at first, but I know she had no choice. She rang her father and he came and found you. He brought you up, Dylan, and kept you safe."

"Why the hell did she run to New York and never come back? She disappeared. I never saw her again."

"Our mother had to hide because if he found her he would have killed her and taken us back. Our lives would have been hell, Dylan. For fuck's sake listen to me for once."

"I would have rather lived with her and known her," Dylan shouted, walking toward him ready to resume the fight. "You got to be loved by her."

"We lived in poverty. She couldn't even tell her own family where she was or get financial help from them in case he found us. He finally caught up with her when we turned fifteen and shot her dead when I was out playing the big man in a gang. I came home to find her lying dead in our crappy little apartment. I lost everything that day. I didn't have it easy. At least you lived in wealth with our grandparents."

Dylan hung his head and then laughed.

"My grandparents had to fight like hell in the courts to keep me. At first I was returned to him for six months. He beat the crap out of me because I wouldn't talk to him and I looked at him the wrong way. One night he nearly killed me. They got me back but it took its toll on our grandfather's health. He was slowly dying of cancer and eventually he died of a heart attack. As soon as I could, I enlisted in the army and I haven't looked back until now."

Drew's heart leapt for them. She hadn't been able to stop herself falling for them both. They were like two halves of one person. It struck her there and then she didn't want to do without either of them. If she loved only one of them the relationship would never be complete.

"This time I am going to win and get the girl and you can do without," Dylan snapped, grabbing hold of Mark to punch him again. His brother raised his own fist, prompting Drew into action.

"For God's sake you are like a couple of little boys having a tantrum. Stop it now."

Both men stopped dead and turned to stare at her in surprise, their fists still in the air.

"I am not to be fought over like a possession and I am not choosing either of you. I decide what is happening here and I think you boys should learn to share again. I want you both," she demanded with authority.

Drew sat back on the leather seat of the Mercedes limousine as it traveled from the Rome airport into the city. Mark sat next to her, Dylan in front. Both men were quiet and reflective. There had been a large discussion after her demand and not all of it amicable. Mark had threatened to spank her for suggesting such a thing and Dylan had been very much against it, threatening to drag her out of the house with him to another safe place where he would confine her naked to a bed until she saw sense. The fighting between the brothers had erupted once more. But her announcement to leave both of them and have nothing more to do with them had the twins reconsidering.

Dylan's mobile rang but Drew couldn't understand a word of Italian he was speaking. It made her nervous and Mark sensed it immediately. He covered her hand with his on the seat and clasped it tightly.

"We will find her, honey. Try to relax. You are already exhausted. I wish you didn't look so pale. I have been so worried about you. Next time make sure you tell me everything."

"You were going to stop me leaving and were intent on keeping me locked up in that lair you call your apartment. I love the way you want to protect me but I was going to go mad sitting there waiting for news," she said, leaning over to give him a quick kiss.

He grinned.

"Next time you try to leave when it isn't safe I am going to whip your ass and tie you to the bed."

The tone in his voice told her he wasn't joking.

"Already done that to her. It works quite well," Dylan mocked. "Alessandra Cavalli has been picked up but she didn't have Eva with her. But before you get too worried, Sumner and our father are not in the country. We've had the FBI hold Sumner on suspicion of money laundering last night. They probably won't find anything. My father is good at tying up loose ends and protecting those that work with him, and for him but it will slow him down getting to Italy. Our father has disappeared off the radar."

"So who has Eva?"

Dylan leaned over and rubbed her leg.

"We are working on it. I won't let you down."

"We won't let you down," Mark corrected.

Drew needed some air.

"Can we please just stop the car? I need some air and normality."

Drew couldn't stop thinking about Eva. All kinds of hideous imaginings kept her precariously close to the edge of hysteria. If she didn't get her back she wasn't sure she could survive. She watched Mark look at Dylan and nod.

"OK. Just for a short while then I want you safe in the hotel. People are looking for you and a team has already started picking up suspects in Venice and Rome on charges of human trafficking. Our father is going to stop at nothing to make sure his investment is safe, not to mention the terrorists he is dealing with. There is a lot at stake here. You are our star witness. The refugee camp manager you contacted who confided in you about the abductions of girls for terrorists on the Italian coast has been killed."

"What? You didn't tell me."

"I thought it wise not to upset or distract you. You have enough to worry about and concentrate on with Eva missing."

"What if the bastard gave Eva to the terrorists? Families give their daughters when they are babies to the family of their prospective husband and make them marry the son as an older child. What if James did that to get back at me? The monster never cared for Eva. He always wanted a son. Oh, my God. Stop the car now!" she shouted. "I can't stand this. I can't breathe. I can't breathe."

She was loosening her seatbelt when Dylan shouted at the driver to stop. The car screeched to a halt among the tourists on a street and she got out quickly, followed by both men. She ran away from them before they could stop her.

13

Drew took refuge in a book shop trying to hide from the men. She wanted time on her own to think. Walking to the back of the shop to keep hidden, she pretended to look at some books. After a short while her mind began to calm a little. That was when she noticed a man watching her with interest. It made her decide it might be prudent to leave the shop. But as she started to walk past him, his hand shot out and settled on her arm.

"Hello. I couldn't help noticing you." The voice was English and refined. "You don't appear to look very well. Can I be of assistance?"

Drew looked at the man. There was something familiar about him she couldn't quite put her finger on. He was tall with dark brown hair, smooth complexion, athletically built which shone through the navy Savile Row suit he wore. He was good looking and definitely wealthy. Blue eyes stared back at her with an amused twinkle in them and something told her to be on her guard.

"No. Thank you. I am just a little tired."

She tried to pull her arm back, but the stranger wasn't letting go and now he was putting his arm around her shoulders as he gripped her arm tighter.

"Let me go."

"I think I should help you get some rest. There are some people who want to talk to you. I can protect you from them, but first you must accept my proposal."

"No. Let me go."

"Let her go, Paul."

It was Mark. He removed Paul's hand from Drew's arm and pushed him away, pulling her to his side. Drew let out the breath she had been holding. Paul folded his arms and grinned. Dylan appeared at Drew's other side.

"Long time, no see, brother."

"Stepbrother."

"What are you doing here, Paul?" Dylan asked. "I thought you would be helping our father sort out his criminal problem."

"I run my own business now. I fancied branching out on my own."

"I doubt that. You are always hanging on Daddy's coattails," Dylan mocked.

"You are just sore you can't find anything to pin on me."

"Oh, I'll get you in one of our cells yet. Mark, get Drew out of here and away from this vermin."

"Who are you? Do you know anything about the whereabouts of my daughter? Tell me now," Drew challenged, feeling her anger rise to the boiling point and fizzle. "What is this proposal you talked about?"

"Come with me and you will find out. I can help you find her. I have contacts that could help you much better than Interdefense can."

"Mark," Dylan was annoyed, pushing his stepbrother away from Drew.

Mark's strong arms wound around Drew's waist and lifted her up and away from Paul. Everyone turned to look and murmur as her legs kicked at the air and she fought to free herself from his hold. Two men in suits appeared at Paul's side.

Drew pulled at Mark's arms, but they refused to let go of her. He didn't put her down until they were a small distance away from the shop and made her sit down on a bench.

She was shaking and her head was spinning with tension pain and dizziness that came upon her quickly. She raised her eyes up at Mark blinking in the strong sunlight.

"Drew, are you all right?" he asked tenderly, bending down to cup her face with his hand. "You look unwell again."

"Why did you stop me talking to him? He could have told me where Eva was."

Mark shook his head.

"My stepbrother is a very dangerous man. He is playing games with you. When I think he could have taken you away. What the hell does he want with you? He deals in everything from drugs to murder, trafficking, prostitution, and gun running. He always manages to evade the law because of his contacts rumored to be in the UK and US governments just like my father. He prides himself on being able to provide whatever the customer wants and acts like a concierge. He has his hand in everything. He no longer works with my father and has set out to be better. I won't have him near you. Are you all right?"

He stroked her cheek and his warming touch melted some of her cold anger.

"I'm fine. Thanks."

"You don't look it. We will take you to the hotel and straight to bed. Eva has to be somewhere in Rome. God, Drew, I would move heaven and Earth to find her for you if I could."

Drew nodded, putting her hand to her head in a vain attempt to somehow stop the spinning in her head. She held his free hand, giving it a quick squeeze.

Dylan arrived. "I don't know what game Paul is playing, but I want him kept away from Drew. I want to get you back to the hotel and you can tell me everything he said to you."

His words faded into the background and the world started to fade.

"Drew, darling." Dylan was holding her slumped form on the bench while Mark called the car over from where the driver had parked it across the street. He put the back of his hand across her forehead.

"You look hot but you don't have a fever. You should be resting in bed. Come on, let's get you there as soon as we can."

He moved to help her stand, but she couldn't appear to manage the feat and her legs buckled. Dylan swept her up into his arms and deposited her in the car.

The car sped past the Coliseum and through the streets of Rome to join the traffic. The scene faded to black and Drew fainted in Mark's arms.

She awoke in Mark's arms. He was carrying her. They were inside a lift in a hotel and the doors were closing. His brother was next to him. Drew blinked her eyes, blearily attempting to take in her surroundings to get her bearings.

"Hey, she's waking up," Mark told Dylan, tightening his hold around her body.

Dylan quickly turned and stroked his fingers through her hair as they walked.

"How are you feeling, little one?" he asked in a soft whisper as though speaking to a child.

"I think I am OK," she answered in a sleepy voice.

"You need some rest and then we will discuss what we are going to do next," Mark said, carrying her out of the deserted lift straight into a large opulent room filled with whites, marble pillars, and light grey suede upholstery.

"I will put her in my bed," Mark said, carrying her through into another room in which a bed draped in sumptuous silver silk sheets was center stage.

The penthouse rooms were oval and in front of the huge bed big enough for four let alone two, there were four tall thin windows hitting the floor around the curved wall dressed in white curtains. They looked out over the city and Drew was sure she caught a glimpse of the Coliseum in the distance. Mark moved toward the bed and laid her down on top of it. Somewhere from below the elevated room, she heard the hoot of taxis and the roar of motorcycles and scooters in the midday traffic.

Dylan swept his hand around the back of her head to lift it off the pillows so he could put them in a better position to support her.

Mark was on the phone ringing for some aspirin and tea.

Both men towered over her in their black business suits, their tall dominant male frames dwarfing her small curved figure lying on the bed. She felt small and vulnerable in their power and loved the way they were making the effort to work together to take care of her.

"I am OK, really. I'd like to get up. There must be something I can do to help find Eva. If I keep busy and focus I will feel better. Paul said he would help me if I accepted his proposal," she told them, sitting up.

"I am having him checked out, Drew. I will find out if he knows anything, but I highly doubt it. He plays games and when I questioned him he didn't appear to know much at all. He knows our father is interested in you and he will simply use you as bait to get in on the action. Try not to worry too much. No way are we letting you up." Dylan was firm in his tone.

Both brothers leaned over and gently pushed her back down onto the pillows. Dylan softened his tone.

"You are safe now. Mark and I will take care of you. Sleep."

"I can take care of myself."

Mark laughed.

"One thing Dylan and I agree on is that you need to be taken in hand for your own good. You are reckless with your safety and you need looking after whether you like it or not. We are going to make this work for you. Neither of us is prepared to let go of you, so you will have to get used to both of us dominating you." Mark caressed his fingers around her jaw and lowered his voice to a caressing whisper. "And you, baby girl, will need to be submissive to both of us. Now do as you are told and sleep or you will take a turn over both of our knees for a spanking."

Drew knew by the resolve on their faces that they meant it.

"Yes, Sirs," she said meekly and turned away from them to sleep. She could almost feel the satisfied conquering smiles on their faces. They turned her back to face them.

"Oh, no. You don't get away that easy, darling. Time to get you undressed," Dylan grinned.

Mark opened her cream blouse, taking his time to undo each pearl button before opening it wide and raising her a little way from the bed to remove it. Her breasts heaved up toward him, aching for his touch. As though to answer the call he swept his hands over the swells making her nipples erect before slipping them underneath her back to undo the catch on her bra. He slid the straps down over her shoulders and exposed the milky mounds. He cupped them lightly and bent to give the tip of each one a quick gentle kiss.

Taking away one of his hands allowed Dylan to replace the hold with his own lifting and confining one plump breast in his palm. Both men squeezed each breast at the same time. Their simultaneous touch was electric, causing Drew to throw her head back on top of the pillows. They flexed their thumbs over the nipples, increasing her arousal before stretching and pulling the teats until she gave a small cry at the intense pain.

Dylan moved his hands down to her full pretty pink skirt and undid the button and zip at the back. He tugged at it, swishing it down her curved thighs until it glided over her pink strappy heels. His hands caressed over her bottom before pulling down her lacy pink thong. He held it still at the tops of her pale cream thighs and smoothed his palms over her bare bottom.

"Beautiful. Such a delicious bottom. I loved it the minute I saw it, Mark. Perfect for spanking when she is a naughty girl," he grinned.

Drew jumped when he suddenly turned her and spanked her bottom with his hand twice. Her flesh stung. Allowed to lie flat on the bed, she opened her mouth to give a light protest but Dylan captured her head and pressed his lips against her own. His kiss was strong and dominant, his tongue pushing and probing, wrestling hers for control until she submitted. That was when she felt Mark catch up the material of her panties and tear them apart and away from her body with his bare hands.

"You won't need these again," he said huskily. "Our baby girl isn't allowed to wear panties unless she is menstruating and that hasn't happened yet," he grinned.

Drew gave a pleasurable purr just like a satisfied kitten against Dylan's lips and a pleasured whimper when Mark strongly held her naked hips. He was now sitting on the side of the bed leaning over her pussy. She could feel his crimson tie brushing the tops of her thighs, tickling her delicate pale skin. Her breath grew short against Dylan's lips when Mark bent to brush his lips over the top of her clit.

"Let's get those legs open and you nice and wide," he whispered as Dylan took hold of both breasts to squeeze them as he continued to suck feverishly on her bottom lip.

With a jolt she felt her legs being roughly parted and the first stroke of Mark's fingers between the folds of her pussy.

"Good girl, nice and wet already. Try her," she heard him tell his brother in a smooth voice.

The way they talked and operated in perfect unison was erotic. They were right—they were really trying. She had every hope they would resolve their difficulties in their new relationship. She couldn't bear to be without either of them.

Every touch was flushing her skin with buttery arousal. She was drenched in their power.

Dylan splayed one of his hands down her stomach and then slid his fingers down through Drew's dampening vagina. His brother circled his fingers' wet tips over her hip and into her bottom. She was shocked when he slipped his finger between the crease and trailed it around the puckered entrance.

"I can't wait to take her here," he grinned.

"Me too," Dylan agreed.

Mark's hands held her hips again and began to move her onto her front.

"I want to inspect you, little one, nothing more. When you begin your life with us you will be inspected every morning and night so we can insure your perfect health, honey. Now be a good girl and let Daddy examine you. You still haven't got your period. Too much stress. Relax."

Drew warmed at his use of words. It made her feel safe, protected, controlled, and guided. The more they took charge of her and her body, the more relaxed and content she became in their hold. She couldn't understand her feelings to be loved by two men at the same time, but they were there and strong. She wanted them to take care of her, to take all of her problems away and bring Eva back to her. She was so tired of fighting on her own. They were offering to do it and all she had to do was to submit and surrender to their rule.

After fighting for control from James for so long, she would never have believed she would have allowed herself to entertain being dominated by two men like this. But then she hadn't expected to let a husband abuse her and confine her in a forced marriage with manipulation and fear. She wanted to be loved and protected.

"Let's have a look at her, Mark," Dylan said, momentarily pushing his middle finger up inside Drew's wet vaginal channel from behind to give her a taste of what was to come.

Dylan's caress was to make her pant but suddenly he removed it. Mark gripped her hips again and used his hold to slide her around the bed until she lay in the middle of it and her pelvis rested at the edge. He put his palm into the small of Drew's and held her down.

Dylan arrogantly opened her buttocks wide and peered into the small hole with his brother. She closed her eyes, feeling the heat of her embarrassment at being so intimately examined, just as she had done when examined by the doctor in Mark's apartment. He pushed his finger wet from her juice a little way into the hole with great care. Drew squirmed and whimpered with gentle discomfort and the sensation of being entered in the dark puckered entrance. His free hand patted her bottom to soothe her and then he removed his finger.

"You're very tight in there, baby girl. Just the way we like it."

Mark inserted his own damp finger just inside the entrance, making her catch her breath.

"But your Daddies will take it nice and slow and won't take you there until you are ready. We know James hurt you there. Time to put you into bed, little girl." Mark's voice was velvet, dark, and seductive.

He slowly raised her up and slipped his arm under her body to turn her over before lifting her up into his arms. Mark waited for Dylan to pull the silk sheet away.

Mark laid her down on the sheet as his brother started loosening his own red tie. He startled her by taking hold of her arms and moving them above her head, clasping them together. Mark held them there with one strong hand, pinning her down onto the bed, trailing his fingers along the ridge of her delicate cheek.

"We want you bound for your first taking together. Nice, secure, and safe, darling. No fear, please. I want you to trust us," Mark told her.

Dylan advanced toward her with his tie and wrapped its fine silk length around her wrists to secure them above her head. Excitement rose in the pit of her stomach at the thoughts of their first lovemaking session together. The pads of Dylan's fingers on his dry hand trailed down to her pussy, between her petal lips, stroking through her growing wetness to soothe, calm, and prepare. He pinched and teased the small bud nestled there and Drew became lost and obedient in arousal, once more completely in their control, moaning out her need scorching the insides of her thighs.

Mark removed his tie and pulled it taut before threading the material through her mouth to gag her.

"Good, she's ready," Mark said, moving over to lie next to her on the other side of the bed while Dylan did the same on the opposite. Propped up in lazy elegance they rested their heads on their hands and cast their eyes possessively over her as though she was a tasty dish. Neither of them had attempted to remove their suits and remained fully clothed, adding to her feeling of vulnerability in their power.

Part of her became confused and a little nervous at the ravenous way their eyes were devouring her and she found herself struggling, moving restlessly on the bed, straining on her bonds. But despite the tinge of fear she experienced at being so confined she couldn't help but purr and moan enjoying the stretched look of her body as it moved trying to free itself from the ties. Her vagina was drenched and her breasts tingled with a fiery, painful need to be held. Her breath came in fits and starts, building the anticipation while they cruelly made her wait for their touch.

Both brothers were captivated. Each caught a breast in their hand and squeezed tightly, flexing their thumbs over the nipples to hold her still. Drew arched her body upward in response, relishing the feeling of being controlled and letting her desire flourish and grow so wantonly.

"There is nothing more exquisite than an aroused woman straining on her bonds while you make her wait to be taken on your own terms at your own pleasure," Mark said to his brother with a twinkle in his eye.

"Apart from draping her naked body over your knee to spank her for being a naughty little girl. Then her vulnerability and submission is breathtaking," Dylan mused. "And you, Drew, are a natural female submissive. We are going to enjoy taking you in hand," he said, leaning over her to press his lips gently to her forehead.

"So, brother, I take it we are in agreement to share little one after all our arguments?" Mark questioned.

"Well, I am not willing to give her up to you and I guess it is the same for you. She is too delectable and exactly what we have both been looking for in a woman for a long time. So I suppose we will both have to lump it and share like we used to."

"I guess we will."

In unison the brothers moved their fingers inside her pussy and stroked. Fire scorched Drew's insides. Dylan moved two of his fingers up inside her channel, stretching as far as he could reach them. She panted, bucking her hips upward, wanting him deeper. She was lost in her desire, bound and gagged for their pleasure and their convenience. Her body moved against the silk sheet, delighting in its seductive caress of her skin as they stoked her need out of control.

"Who is going to have the pleasure of mounting her first and sealing our agreement?" Mark asked.

"Before that, we need to do something else. We need to spank our little girl and let her know we won't tolerate her allowing herself to be abused again by a man like James Sumner. She needs rescuing from herself and some stern discipline if we are to make her fit, well, and encourage healthy self-esteem in her. Don't you agree?" he asked in a stern voice, a faint trace of humor lining his words.

"I agree."

With a whimper Drew found herself being roughly turned over. Mark raised her bottom into the air, forcing her to bend her knees but keep her chest on the bed, her tied wrists held out in front of her. It appeared the boys wanted firm discipline to be part of her healing process. The first time Mark spanked her over his desk in his apartment had shocked her, but now she was beginning to understand it was wielded with love and she welcomed it as a new component of her life to guide and protect her from her own recklessness.

Dylan pressed the top half of her body down onto the sheet, squashing her breasts into it.

"Face down, little one," he ordered. Eager to please, Drew rushed to obey.

She wasn't sure why she did but it was the commanding tone in his voice that made her act. It was hard to resist and every time one of them spoke to her that way she dampened heavily between her thighs. It felt natural to be told what to do, not like James had done but to be ruled with loving intention was pleasurable and deeply arousing. She was beginning to crave their dominance.

The nagging doubting voice in the back of her mind would try its best to remind her of her apparent error in judgment and thinking. But with determination she closed the voice down and allowed herself to surrender to her own wishes.

Dylan moved off the side of the bed while Mark continued to lie next to her, stroking his fingers through her hair. But they were removed when Dylan caught the back of her hair up into a ponytail and roughly tugged it to make her head rise and fall backwards. He pressed his palm into the middle of her back.

"Take a deep breath and then let it out slowly for me, darling," he said in a deep, melodic voice. A whoosh of air sounded through her ears and the first strike of his hard palm made contact with her bare bottom.

She groaned against the tie in her mouth and tried to put her head down, but Dylan was pulling her head up firmly by the ponytail he used to steady her for spanking. She was aware of Mark kneeling on the bed with him. His hand closed around Drew's throat and held her firmly. Dylan concentrated his punishing strikes on one buttock, leaving the other free for his brother to lash with his own hand. The men picked up a rhythm. First one would strike, then the other, until Drew was whimpering and gentle tears brushed her cheeks. By the time they diverted their attention to the tender backs of her thighs she was sobbing out all of her pain and worry over Eva and her life with James releasing in a torrent with the double punishment.

Dylan lowered her head back down and smoothed his palm

comfortingly over her burning soreness before bending to kiss the pain on one buttock away. His brother followed suit, bestowing his kiss over his own cheek. Then he moved back on the bed beside her, covering her naked body in the top sheet. Neither spoke. They trailed soothing butterfly kisses along her back and hair, moving their fingers between her thighs to her pussy both coaxing and teasing the fire still dwelling there, rekindling the embers, each sliding a finger up inside her channel to fondle the center of pleasure until she could hold back no longer and she came strongly, crying out her release against the gag in her mouth.

"Good girl, get that emotion out. You did well, baby girl," Mark whispered.

They worked together to turn her over flat, making sure the sheet was tucked around her before removing the gag and bindings. They placed their arms around her on top of the sheet and held her, pressing their bodies protectively close.

"This is your safe place, little girl, between us. When you are fearful or upset we will put you to bed and hold you until you feel safe and loved again. I have an inkling this is going to be a long journey for you, kitten. There is a lot of pain to come out. We will help you heal," Mark informed her in a concerned tone, kissing her bare shoulder. "Now sleep, then we will make love to you and seal our agreement."

14

Drew woke from a comfortable slumber a couple of hours later. She hadn't felt this relaxed for a very long time. The feel of the silk sheets stroking her naked body with every movement was once more enticing. She turned sensuously against the material, moaning softly at the newfound peace and safety she felt.

To her surprise she wasn't alone in the room. On one side of the bed Dylan sat on a chair and on the other side Mark was doing the same. She was guarded on both sides and any fleeting ideas she might conjure of just slipping out of the room was completely out of the question. She smiled, feeling protected. They must have been watching over her as she slept.

She belonged to them now. Willingly she had given herself to them both and there was no going back. The very idea made her feel a little nervous, but the small amount of dampness beginning to slicken the tops of her thighs between her legs at her thoughts betrayed her acceptance at being owned by them both.

They were talking in whispered voices over her and hadn't yet seen she was awake. Mark was looking at something on a tablet. She decided to listen in and see what they were talking about in earnest and closed her eyes tight, faking sleep.

"I thought she was waking up there," Dylan said, standing up over her, pausing their conversation.

Drew felt the brush of his fingers on her cheek. Every time one of them touched her, warm softness covered her body like a nurturing blanket and she became naturally pliant and obedient to their wishes. She wanted to obey them and reap the delicious rewards they would bestow on her for being a good girl. It was fast becoming a compulsion.

Dylan leaned over her to lower his lips to her forehead.

"Poor little girl, in so much pain. Daddy will look after you."

Mark was suddenly on his feet. She listened to him walk over to the bed and through her closed lids she saw his shadow descend over her. His fingers wove through her hair hanging free on her shoulders.

"Both of your Daddies will look after you and see to your every need."

Drew wanted to smile at the jealousy the twin brothers were displaying. There was no need—she was in love with them both.

"She reminds me of our mother and the way our father used to treat her. She deserves better. Is it the same for you?" Mark asked.

Dylan's voice was somber when he spoke.

"Yes, she does. He is going to come looking for her himself at some point. He's been stopped from ending her a few times now. He will want to take control of her demise himself now. He is never going to stop until he has destroyed her. We have to keep her safe."

"I know. What the hell is Paul up to? What does he want with her? He has been following us around."

"Yes. You know Paul, he always wants what we have. Maybe he thinks he can use her as a bargaining chip with Father?"

"Did you see the way he was looking at Drew?"

"He was very taken with her. He looked like he wanted to consume her."

"It makes me sick."

"Every time I look for something to bring him in for, there is nothing. I am worried for Drew. He is using Eva to taunt her. I have put a tail on him."

"I am frightened to leave her alone."

"Me, too. So we won't. At least one of us must be present by her side at all times."

"She will get angry."

"Tough."

"Agreed. We won't let you end up like our mother," Mark said, continuing to stroke his fingers through her hair.

She could hear real pain behind the words.

"I am so glad we found her. She's everything I...we want, delicate, fragile, beautiful. So very beautiful. I can't wait to be inside her again," Dylan confessed.

"I feel the same way. Who gets to take her first?" Mark was determined to be first.

She could hear it in his dominant tone and he clearly expected his brother to capitulate. Dylan gave a small laugh.

"You always believe you have first right to everything as the oldest. You were born three minutes before me."

She felt the touch of Dylan's fingers on her cheek again. "Maybe we should fight for the privilege?" He spoke softly but there was a possessive menace lacing his tone.

"I wouldn't do that to her. I don't want her to wake up seeing us fight for the right to mount and claim her first either verbally or physically in this new relationship. I think she has seen enough of that."

"I hate to admit it, but you are right. I will allow you to go first, older brother," Dylan finished sarcastically. "Just by going first does not mean you will get to capture all of her heart."

"You always have to have the last word. Thank you. You heard her—we both have her heart. And when Drew says something she never goes back on it. It is one of the things I love about her." He paused and then tentatively spoke again.

"I want to establish some of my own rules I need her to abide by in her submission. I need total obedience from her and I won't settle for anything else. We need to set our own boundaries and rules so she does not become confused or hurt."

"Knowing us, they will be exactly the same."

"Even so. Anyway, you never know for once we might find a difference. Drew is too precious a find to lose. This has to be done properly or not at all," Mark said sternly.

"I agree. I am not going to lose her."

"We will help her every step of the way to get over her abusive relationship with James and find Eva. Now let's wake her." Mark was suddenly impatient. "I want to begin her submission training. We need to make her wear a collar. I want to see her in one as soon as possible. There is nothing more delectable than a woman kneeling naked in a collar at your feet."

"Like I said, you can take the lead on this occasion but don't dare to try and push me out or I will come down hard on you. Do you understand, Mark?"

The threat was clear and Drew dampened more at the notion of feeling possessively owned by the two alpha brothers who fought for the right to make her their own. But she couldn't help feeling a little perturbed at the idea of wearing a collar and kneeling. Could she really allow herself to do that? Wasn't that more abuse? She wasn't sure in her mind, yet her body had other ideas. It melted and breathed an unconditional yes to being harnessed in a collar and made to submit at the brothers' feet. Maybe this had always been in her.

"Yes, I think it is time she was awake or our little kitten won't sleep very well tonight."

Drew kept her eyes closed, wondering how she was about to be awoken. Dylan's shadow moved away and she heard him sit down in the white padded chair on the other side of the bed to watch.

Mark sat down on the side of the bed. She held her breath when the sheet they had covered her in to sleep like a baby was gently lifted. The seductive brush of Mark's hand on her thigh signaled the beginning of her submission training. He circled his fingers along the soft skin lining her thigh, then traveled to the side of one round juicy ripe buttock. Restlessly she shifted and moaned, lifting and separating her thighs.

"Good girl, nice and wide for me," he whispered, still believing she was asleep.

His palm flattened and the heat that still pulsed from her spanking before she was put to bed for sleeping warmed his hand.

"Such a lovely bottom. Not a skinny, bony one. Just perfect. I love the sound it makes when you slap it. Time to wake up."

Mark's voice was a smooth velvet whisper and it matched his caress that cascaded from her bare bottom round over one silky thigh to plunge downward. His stroke through the plump wet folds of Drew's vagina was expertly executed and designed to heavily arouse.

"Already wet, little girl," he said with surprise. "I wonder if our little kitty has already stirred and woken. Perhaps she is feigning sleep so she can eavesdrop on us."

Drew's heart began to thud. She felt another spanking coming on and feared for her already burning bottom.

"Let's see if I am right."

Drew's eyes flew open when Mark's hand left her vagina and in one fluid moment pulled the sheet from the bed to expose her naked body to both brothers' eyes. Her pelvis bucked upwards, thrusting her wet pussy into the air and Mark was quick to take advantage. He cupped the wet V-shape and spanked it hard with his hand, making her yelp out loud. Two more perfectly aimed slaps that caught the tip of her clit were to follow.

He leaned over her to hold her shoulder and keep her firmly down on the bed so she could not prevent him from disciplining her, spanking her sex some more. Dylan stood up to watch, an amused smile curling his sexy lips. His eyes appeared taken with the way her breasts bounced on her chest with each firm swat. Drew's yelps blossomed into pants and surprised moans of pleasure.

The strikes had stung at first. But the brief slap of pain had begun to be followed by drenching wetness that was now coating his palm. Mark ended her short punishment by cupping her pussy and squeezing it. Drew started to ache with need.

Mark leaned over her again, his lips inches from her own.

"I think it is time you learned some of my rules, honey. No eavesdropping. There is no need for it. Dylan and I will share everything with you. We will keep nothing from you. We both want your full submission to our own distinctive rules as well as joint ones we will make. We need you to fully trust us for this relationship to work. I can understand you have probably been used to hiding, anticipating, and fearing with James and found need to eavesdrop on him to work out his next move with you. But you will need to cultivate trust in us. We will never abuse it."

She stared at him, watching his lips move closer. He smiled, watching her taking a breath to calm her excitement at his closeness. His middle finger in the hand that so firmly held her pussy pushed at the entrance to her channel and penetrated it. Her body rose up against his hand.

She hadn't spoken yet and it was clear he was waiting for her to confirm that she had understood him.

"Yes, I understand."

"Yes, I understand, Daddy," he corrected.

Drew licked her bottom lip, feeling it dry with a small amount of nervousness. Mark was mesmerized by the action.

"Yes, Daddy," she said demurely, her eyelashes involuntarily fluttering at the strength of his dominance and the pleasure he was creating with the thrust of his finger in and out of her.

"Good girl," he whispered, kissing her gently. "Now, I think it is time you showed us you are ready to submit. You seemed to sleep well. Is that true?"

"Yes, Daddy."

He nodded with approval. His dark eyes bored into her.

"Stand and kneel at my feet, little one."

Drew took another breath, not sure if she could do as he asked. Mark took his finger from her sex and made sure she saw him slipping his finger between his lips to taste her.

"Very nice," he smiled, sucking at his finger. "I look forward to tasting more."

Mark straightened and picked up her small hand to cradle it in his large one. He gently tugged on it to pull her up from the bed. He led her naked body away from the bed as though parading her around. The simple act made her feel like a queen. The twins cast their eyes upon her small curved form with appreciation, making her blush. She'd never had much confidence in her body, always feeling afraid and ashamed of her curves and lamenting she couldn't have a tall, thin, boyish body. But here and now she was beginning to feel happier her shape and form was delighting the men and it was not being condemned.

Mark smiled and brought her hand to his lips when they reached a space in the floor next to the sofa in the lounge area. He kissed it.

"Kneel," he commanded with a firm voice, pointing his finger at the floor.

Drew looked down with fear, wondering if she could allow herself to kneel. But that strange compulsion to please and feel submissive began to lower her frame onto the soft blue grey carpet. Her body felt warm and pliant as though it was melting at the command she had been given. There was such strength in Mark's voice she found it hard to resist.

Drew glanced at Dylan who was now to her side as she knelt. Her eyes widened when she saw him holding a leather collar, leash, and rope.

Both men were in command and she was to show her acceptance of their rule in turn. Licking her bottom lip with the curl of her wet tongue, heart beating fast she looked up at the tall dark handsome dominant man standing immaculately dressed in his black suit and tie just like his brother whose feet she now knelt obediently at feeling vulnerable and helpless. Pleasure flooded her sex and tightened the tips of her nipples. They looked down with approval at her.

Mark bent to tuck his fingers underneath her chin and raised it.

"That wasn't too hard now, was it?" he whispered. "Put your hands behind your back and cross them. You must be bound. This is just the beginning of your submission training, little one, and I expect your obedience at all times or you will find yourself over my knee to have that delicious pert plump bottom of yours whipped or paddled until you understand I am in charge. Do I make myself clear?"

"Yes, Daddy."

Mark moved toward Drew, resting one of his hands on top of her shoulders. His other hand took the silken rope from his brother.

"Time to learn Mark's rules," he said, placing the rope in front of her.

He wound it fast around Drew's breasts, encouraging them to push out of the rope bra. Then he moved it down her lightly curved abdomen, easing it between her thighs and making her give a small cry when he guided it up between the swollen wet lips of her vulva. His palm pressed into her back, setting her skin alight with desire with the firmness of the touch he used to bend her forward and up off sitting on her ankles so he could thread the rope up between the crease of her bottom.

Mark skilfully fed the rope back around to her front to secure her wrists.

"Let's put the collar on you."

Drew shifted, feeling the rope rub through her pussy and over her anal entrance, helping to make her slicker and aching for penetration. She couldn't help but marvel at the intricate way Mark had taken time to work the rope around her as though it were an art form. She was now in a position in which she had no choice but to trust the brothers to take care of her.

There was an intoxicating smell of leather as Mark suddenly sheathed her throat and neck in a high leather collar. He fastened it at the back, forcing a gasp from her lips as he did. It felt like a possessive male hand around her throat.

From the middle of the collar there was a small steel ring protruding. Mark bent and fixed the long leather leash to the ring. He pulled it taut and forced Drew's head back, allowing her to feel the full effect of his mastery over her.

"Don't be frightened, little one," he told her, running his thumb over her pink bottom lip. "All we do to you now is to help you embrace pleasurable submission. We will never hurt you," he told her, pressing his thumb between her lips and demanding entry.

Obediently Drew opened her mouth and allowed him to insert his thumb. He pulsed it in and out, generating a curious passion for her to suck on it as though it were his penis.

"I think our baby girl is ready," Mark grinned.

Every time she rocked on her knees the silken rope rubbed at her wet sex and against the small hole between her bottom, building her desire to be penetrated to fever pitch. Her pussy throbbed, wishing it could suck the rope up inside her and ride it to satisfaction.

"Good, because I am not sure I can wait any longer to fuck her," Dylan said. There was amusement in his tone. "She looks so beautiful and helpless. Just the way we always want her to be."

Mark removed his thumb from Drew's mouth and pulled the lead on the collar taut. He tugged it twice and instructed her to shuffle forward on her knees. She did as she was bid, knowing fine well what was about to happen. He unzipped his trousers. He wasn't wearing any underwear and he pulled out his hard cock. Mark pulled harder on the lead and forced Drew's head forward. He guided his penis between her pouting lips and thrusted inside her mouth.

"Suck," he commanded. "And mind you, drink every last drop," he ordered, turning the leash around his hand to pull it tighter and keep her down on his penis. He pumped slow into her mouth at first, reaching to the back of her throat and then drawing out at a sedate pace. She suckled on his length and the droplets of nectar that sprung from its tip.

Dylan sat down on the sofa to view the proceedings. She was on full display: bound, collared, and leashed, increasing the potency of her helplessness and their dominance still fully clothed in their matching designer suits.

With a loud sigh of satisfaction, Mark increased the speed of his movement inside her mouth and thrusted his cock deep until it nudged at the back of her throat and induced her gagging reflex. He held his penis there for a moment, waiting for the small urge to gag, relax, and accept defeat. Then he pushed a little further until the orifice was filled and consumed by his dominant length.

Desire pooled in Drew's pussy, soaking the rope.

"God, you look beautiful. So alluring and enticing bound and kneeling," Mark said, pulling the leash even tighter until she felt her head move a little to one side as he pumped in and out of her mouth at a cruel pace.

Drew licked and sucked him like an ice-cream cone, flicking the tip of her tongue over the smooth dome of his cock then grazing her teeth lightly over it its smooth surface.

"That's wonderful, baby girl. Just the way Daddy likes it. Suck harder. Take me as deep as you can."

Drew obeyed, feeling Mark's other hand rest on the back of her head forcing her down onto his cock in unison with the leash. His penis jumped and throbbed with the persistent stroke of her tongue. He twisted the leash at the same time as he pulled on her hair to now direct her head slightly backward. He was close. She could tell by his panting and grunting. His cock twitched inside her mouth and all of a sudden he was cumming, filling her mouth to the brim with thick soft warm seed.

Drew had never swallowed before removing her mouth quickly when forced to act for James. Instinctively she tried to move away, but another sharp tug on the leash kept her in firm position and she was made to swallow every last salty drop. Mark's dominance over her at that moment was strong, and being held so firmly in place made her understand his authority. Instead of trying to move away she halted her movement and became eager to please him, swallowing every last drop.

Finally he was empty and the last of his seed slid down her throat to warm her stomach. Mark stayed inside her mouth, stroking the back of her head.

"Wonderful, kitten. But I am only partially satisfied. By the end of this evening I will need to be inside your pussy."

He looked down at Drew, commanding her attention.

"Another rule for you to learn, little one. I will take you whenever and wherever I want. It is my right and privilege as long as it is safe and you are adequately protected. If I need you to go down on me, you will do so without question and darling…"

Mark's fingers lifted from the back of her head to raise her chin.

"You will always swallow every last drop."

"Yes, Daddy."

Slowly Mark pulled himself out of her mouth and dropped the leash. He zipped himself back up. Drew sat quiet and still awaiting his next instruction.

"She performed well," his twin remarked from his chair where he elegantly slouched.

"To perfection. Our little kitten has a good technique. I recommend you try it," he said with a grin.

"I will. Does baby girl need a drink?"

"Yes. I think some water would be a good idea."

Mark knelt down and caught the back of her head to kiss her lips.

"That was really breathtaking," he whispered. "Now for some more training."

15

Drew expected one of the twins to feed the water to her lips but she was to receive another shock. Mark marched past her to the small fridge in the corner next to a desk set up with office equipment to retrieve a bottle of Evian. But he didn't pour it into a glass. He took one of the saucers from the cups on the table arranged for coffee or tea and poured it into one of them before returning.

He placed it on the floor directly in front of her mouth.

"Bend, kitten, and drink from the saucer."

She stared at him, horrified. He smiled gently with reassurance.

"Drink, little one. There is nothing to be afraid of. You have no idea how sexy it is to watch a woman lap water from a saucer like a kitten. This is part of being a submissive. Have no reservations. This is what we expect from you. Submission is required in everything we ask of you and I know it seems daunting to you now, but it will come easily in time, especially to one who is a natural submissive. Now, drink or do I have to make you? Would you prefer me not to give you any choice?"

Drew couldn't quite bring herself to take the plunge and lower her body and mouth to the saucer. It didn't fit as easily as the rest of her training. It was full submission. Yet desire pulsed and stirred in her vagina at the thought. This was what she wanted, so why was it suddenly becoming difficult?

Mark stroked her cheek.

"Mark's rules," he began. "Never be afraid to tell me what is wrong or what you are unsure about. You will be listened to with respect and guided in the proper manner."

When he talked to her of his rules Mark was formal, his voice clipped and clear so there was no room for misunderstanding. It gave her strong reassurance and made her feel safe. His voice was always soothing, respectful, and gentle. When he spoke, it was like having a warm soft velvet blanket placed around her.

"I just feel unsure about this. I want to try it and take pleasure in obeying you, but I feel afraid I will find it demeaning. I shouldn't allow myself to like this kind of thing..." She trailed off listening to her words.

Here she was again keeping her own tight leash on her needs and desires. She had been doing it for too long and now it was a bad habit. If she wanted to submit in every sense of the word and take pleasure and protection in their domination over her, what was wrong with that? What was wrong with being different and not the woman everyone expected her to be? When was she going to let go?

"I want to…" she repeated. "But I am not sure I can let go and allow myself. "Perhaps if…"

"I gave you no choice? Guided you gently and carefully into letting go? Like I did when I made you swallow my seed? Is that what you want, little one?" he asked her seriously.

"Yes. Yes, it is." She tried to say it with complete conviction.

"Then your wish is my command," he answered, picking up the leash again.

"Down, girl and drink," he said carefully, pulling the lead to direct her head downward.

Drew felt the weight of his eyes on her the whole time watching for signs of discomfort or rebellion, but she responded well to his authority and dipped her head at the guide of the leash. He repeated the action until her lips skimmed the surface of the water.

Drew looked down at her reflection in the water and faltered for a moment, questioning herself once more. The whole thought process was leaving her in turmoil, but she was to be jerked from it when Mark reached behind her and gave her naked bottom two sharp slaps. Crying out, she quickly lapped at the water and drank hungrily, forced to keep her posture in the right position and rely on Mark guiding her with leash to keep her steady.

"Good girl, that's better," he told her softly.

Mark stroked her hair, watching her drink.

"I think some quiet contemplation time would be good for you, Drew. It will allow you to sort out some of those thoughts about submitting to a man. Then I will give you a nice bath and dress you for the party we are going to take you tonight. Do you like dancing, little one?"

"A party? But I thought we were going to stay here and wait for news of Eva? I'm not sure…"

"Hush. This party has been planned for a while. I was going to bring you here anyway. But you left, remember?"

She grimaced, wondering if he would ever stop being annoyed she'd left the apartment without telling him.

"It is a fundraiser I hold every year in different countries to highlight the plight of women suffering from domestic violence, abuse, and rape. It is a charity I named after my mother, the Carrie Dexter Foundation. It just so happens it is happening in Rome this year. I thought you could speak and make an appeal for anyone to come forward with information about Eva's whereabouts. Dylan has already approved it. It will be televised all over the world."

Tears gathered in Drew's eyes. "Yes. Yes I would like that. Thank you."

Mark smiled. "We will be with you. Now keep drinking. You haven't had enough to drink all day. That's it."

"In case you may be wondering what you are going to wear I have that all sorted," Mark said, bending down to watch her lap at the water again. He trailed his fingers over the tip of one nipple underneath her. "I have just called downstairs and arranged for the boutique to show me some dresses and shoes. I will pick some out for you. I have a good eye for that kind of thing," he grinned and pulled at the teat. Drew gave a gentle moan, becoming conscious of the weight of the rope upon her breasts once more before she took another drink.

"Shouldn't I be there to pick my own dress out?"

"Mark and Dylan's rules. From now on we choose your dresses, panties, bras, and stockings. We don't believe in ladies wearing trousers. They are more pretty and enticingly vulnerable in dresses," Mark said in a seductively calming voice designed to thwart any female objection she might have had at him choosing her clothes. "Besides, when we want to take you we simply have to lift your dress and enter you at will. Panties will be a small luxury for you when we allow it or you are menstruating like I said, not a necessity."

"I'm not sure about that," she snapped, lifting her head from the water.

"Well, you will have to be, darling. From now on that's the way your life is going to be. That is the way you have chosen it to be. Let us ease you into it just like you asked," Dylan said from his seat.

Annoyance swelled at the top of her stomach. She was going to have a problem with that. She would be wearing exactly what they said when they said. Wasn't that taking too much freedom away from her? She had to hope they had good taste in dressing a woman or she was in even more trouble. Judging by the clothes they wore and the fact money was no object she hoped they would do her justice and not buy her anything outlandish or something that made her uncomfortable to wear.

"I will try," she said, swallowing her pride.

"Don't worry, you will be pleased with the results. Everything we buy you will fit you and your personality. You are a classy lady, Drew, and class is what you will get, baby girl."

Mark let go of her nipple and stroked her bottom.

"I think she's had enough water. Let's relax for a while and give her some time to think about what we expect from her," Mark said, forcing her to rise with a tug on the leash.

"Stand for me, little one. Dylan, please order some sandwiches and tea. Kitten needs some food. She fell asleep before the tea was sent up earlier."

Mark led her to one of the sofas by a small white marble

fireplace.

"Kneel again."

Becoming more accustomed to his stern orders, she knelt at his feet. He took a red cushion from the chair and placed it on the floor in front of her.

"Put your face on the cushion and thrust your bottom up into the air so I can gaze upon you while I sit and read my reports for the office before your tea arrives, little one."

With trepidation, Drew leaned forward and put her face down on the cushion.

The twins stood over her, making her feel self-conscious under their careful scrutiny.

"There is something missing," Mark said, bending to smooth his hand over one buttock and then between the crease, making Drew jump.

"Yes," Dylan agreed. "She needs to be plugged."

Drew gulped as he raised himself and left the room for a moment.

He fetched a tub of lubricant and a shiny anal plug with a small diamond on the end.

Dylan came over to view the proceedings. She felt the brush of Mark's hand across her back. He was kneeling behind her, his free hand pulling open the crease of her buttocks to place his thumb over the hole. She whimpered a little when he pushed his cool wet lubricated thumb gently into the entrance of her anus.

"Shh, kitten. Everything is all right," he whispered, brushing his lips lightly over one bare buttock. "Daddy will be careful. I won't hurt you. Just relax and continue being obedient."

Dylan's hand rubbed gently down the length of her back as though he were stroking the flanks of a thoroughbred. It made her feel adored and calmer.

"OK, baby girl, this will be over in a moment and then you can relax and look forward to this evening. We want to show you off," Mark said with pride, making her heart leap with joy.

"I think being gagged might help, little one," Dylan suggested, undoing his tie.

It swished out from around his collar and a second later he was pressing the red silk between her lips. Willingly she accepted its forced invasion into her mouth, tipping up her head with parted lips.

Mark moved his middle finger deep inside her dark channel, twisting it gently to make it stretch and widen to accommodate the plug. The small nerve endings in her channel complained at first, making her rock her bottom, but Mark gripped a buttock to hold her still and made her endure the initial discomfort until it eased. He picked up the steel butt plug and lubricated it then he positioned it at the entrance of her anus. Dylan continued to caress her body and gently pulled on her leash.

She gasped with the feel of the cool gel and then the plug was invading her bottom. Dylan continued to hold her leash to keep her in place as the plug continued its path inside. She bleated a little more, disturbed by the strange feeling of having her anal cavity penetrated by something other than a cock rather than the light pain. Her nerve endings tingled once more as Mark pushed further and deeper, forcing them to submit and stretch the channel. Eventually it was inserted and the small jewel protruded from her bottom.

Mark patted her bottom just like his brother had a habit of doing when she had impressed him.

"Perfect. Very pretty. Now face-down on the cushion so that we can admire you while we do some work and wait for the food. Then I will go downstairs and choose some clothes for you."

Mark sat reading reports on one end of the sofa, her leash resting over his lap while his brother sat in a chair on the other side and talked on his mobile. She remained positioned for their viewing pleasure.

When the tea and sandwiches arrived, she was made to drink the tea from the saucer and lap it while they stroked her like a kitten before she was untied and allowed to eat.

That evening the brothers positioned Drew in the middle of the Mercedes with Mark on one side and Dylan on the other. The sexy silk fitted evening dress felt amazing on her curved figure. She had worn pretty evening dresses before, but this one was special. It felt like a million dollars.

The chauffeur opened the door and Dylan got out first, his beady eyes checking for danger before he allowed her out. He wore a microphone in his ear and talked to the other agents hidden amongst the throng of people around the red carpet leading into the theater. Drew's heart began to thud. She'd been given time to prepare a small speech and plead for information before going out. As a journalist the words had come easy, but all these people made her nervous. Camera lights flashed in her eyes, making her feel dizzy again. She took a sharp breath, prompting both brothers to view with her with concern.

"Drew, are you all right?" Dylan asked, resting his hand on her arm after helping her out of the car.

Heat flushed over her skin and every nerve ending in her body tingled with anxiety. She was about to be put on show in a major way.

"I'm fine," she lied. "Just a bit anxious. There are so many people."

"Relax. You are beautiful and everyone is going to adore you and they will listen. We are hoping for some results from your request for information," Dylan said, trailing his fingers along her neck.

He leaned over to whisper in her ear. His breath made her body shiver with pleasure as it blew across her earlobe.

"Just remember who you belong to when the men at this party come around trying to take you from us," he grinned. "Or we might have to lock you up in your room to keep you safe from predators, little one. We are not going to lose you to anyone."

Mark fastened his tuxedo jacket after alighting from the other side and made his way around to them. Both men took hold of one of Drew's arms and led her along the carpet as the cameras flashed like crazy at them.

Mark made her pose for photographs, walking down the carpet to stop at intervals to answer calls from the press from all over the world and the paparazzi.

They carried on down the carpet toward a film crew. Drew's dramatic heartbeat increased when she glanced into the crowd and homed in on someone. Paul Dexter was staring back, grinning at her.

Dylan spoke to his agents and pointed at two of them who

moved into the crowd of onlookers toward Paul and started to pull him away. Dylan swept his arm around Drew's waist, forcibly turning her to face the other way so she would not be looking in his direction and moved her along the carpet.

Mark squeezed her hand and whispered, "A joint rule. We will always keep you safe and protected."

He brushed Drew's cheek with a quick kiss, sending the cameras flashing even more. Dylan didn't appear amused by Mark's declaration of ownership and planted his own on her opposite cheek, clearly unabashed to tell the world she also belonged to him. The cameras went wild.

Mark began talking to the TV crew about his charity before the parade of international film stars and wealthy followed them. There was heavy interest in Drew and the surprise speech she would be giving.

The next thing she knew, she was being marched into the large theater, whose large hall had been converted into a ballroom for the night. Her feet were barely touching the ground. Her anxiety increased. They were afraid for her safety.

"Keep hold of her," Dylan said firmly to his twin, gently pushing Drew at Mark. "I have just heard our father has been seen in the building. They are looking for him now."

"Don't worry, I am not letting her go anywhere."

Mark circled her waist with his hands and moved her into the corner of the glass-paneled lobby, almost lifting her there. He stood in front and faced her. His grip tightened on her waist as he protectively sheltered her from view with his body. Two Interdefense agents came to stand in front of them as he watched his brother stride across the lobby to talk to two others.

She felt the trail of his fingers gently down her cheek before he cupped the side of her face.

"We have been waiting for our father to turn up. There is nothing to be afraid of. This was just another way to flush him out."

"I gathered that."

"But we will keep you safe. I promise."

He sighed and pressed the back of his fingers against her cheek in an effort to give her comfort. Briefly she closed her eyes, warming to the softness of his touch again, feeling the shake in her body begin to recede with his closeness. Yet she still yearned for Dylan to return. She was fast coming to feel distressed without either brother's comforting presence.

But she shivered when she saw Paul emerge in a tuxedo amid the throng in the lobby. The man was coming straight toward them. The agents stepped in front of him and the man accompanying him.

"There is nothing to hold the bastard on," Mark hissed. "I want to warn him off. Stay behind me and do not move or so help me, honey I will take my belt off and whip your bare ass in front of all of these people. Another of Mark's rules. Always obey or expect to have a sore red ass all the time. Paul is dangerous around women and I don't like the way he is looking at you."

Mark put both hands on her waist again and moved her back against the glass behind him before he turned to face his brother and asked the agents to step aside.

"Paul, what the hell are you doing here? What do you want? I told you to keep away."

"I thought I would just check in on you both and your girl. I can still help you find Eva if you are interested," he said, tilting his head to look behind Mark at Drew.

"Stop lying to her. We know you know nothing. Get out before I have you dragged out in front of the cameras."

Drew moved around from behind Mark's back, hoping to learn more from Paul. He made her curious but highly nervous. But the billionaire put his hand behind his back neatly catching hold of her waist and pushed her behind him again.

People were starting to watch and murmur. Drew was starting to feel glad of Mark's tall, muscled, athletic frame determined to hide and protect her in the confined space.

"You need to leave. You wouldn't want to embarrass yourself yet again when you get thrown out of here on your ass."

"Always causing an argument. I will leave. But Drew, think about my offer. I have many contacts that can help."

"Get out. Throw him out."

The agents took a step toward him and closed ranks. Paul held up his hands.

"OK, I am leaving."

The man moved away but there was a new threat standing near them. James Sumner was watching the agents guide Paul out of the building from a distance. Drew found the tension in her body change into anger. She'd had enough of being threatened, and she glared at Sumner disgusted at the fear she felt when he was near. She watched Dylan appear in front of him to remonstrate him. She had to get away and have some space from everyone just for a short while.

Her first inclination was to run to the bathroom, but she couldn't find the rest rooms and instead she spied another set of doors leading out to the side of the building. With a concerted push, she moved Mark away from her and bolted, lifting her long dress up as she did so and disappeared into the crowd. Panic was rising inside her fast and she just wanted to be able to breathe. Stumbling outside, she took in a large gulp of air, feeling relief.

This was the point when she could make a run for it, disappear into the streets of Rome, and not be seen again. She could hunt down Eva on her own. No one would find her and she could finally be free from Sumner. She glanced back, expecting to find the brothers behind her ready to change her mind. But so far she had evaded them. Did she really want to leave them both?

The very idea of leaving them made her want to cry. The pleasure she felt with the twins was exquisite. There was no other adequate word to describe it. When she thought about leaving and running along the busy Roman street toward the Coliseum she could see in the distance again she was incredibly sad. She'd planned to find Eva alone, but she needed help. For once she had to trust someone and allow them to help her or she would lose everything precious in her life.

The internal dialogue continued but was interrupted when the glass doors were flung open. Mark and Dylan moved out onto the street to stand with her.

Mark was furious and his handsome twin brother's eyes were flashing wild with fear and anger.

"God we were so worried," Mark said, firmly taking her arm to pull her to him. "Why did you run away? Did you see James? Why are you crying?" he asked, sweeping his arms around her directing her head to his chest, his anger dispersing into concern as he held her.

There was genuine fear in his tone. Dylan placed his hand on the top of her back above his brother's arms and rubbed it.

Her tone was shaky and pleading. "Yes, and I just wanted some air and to think."

"Hey, relax. We understand," Mark told her as though he had heard her thoughts. "There is no need to feel afraid of us. I can hear it in your voice. We aren't him," he told her, kissing her cheek. "You sound like our mother did with our father. I can't bear it. Neither of us will have you afraid of us."

Dylan pressed his body close to her back and rubbed her shoulders. She was deliciously sandwiched between the two and felt secure. Her shaking calmed.

Mark tilted her chin upward and caught her gaze. He was smiling but his voice became firm and commanding.

"However, little one, you will need to be schooled with a spanking for running away when we were trying to protect you. Mark's rules: Always obey my instructions on your protection. I do not want you leaving my side again. These are the rules you agreed to accept, baby girl, and if you disobey them there will be consequences."

Drew's pussy stirred with moist need. She wanted to be disciplined in the arousing, loving way they used to rule her as her dominants. She needed and craved their control. Nothing made her feel more loved. It was a paradox. Here she was trying to escape a husband who wanted to control her with put-downs and physical abuse, yet she wanted to be mastered by the brothers, brought to kneeling in return for being loved, adored, even worshiped on some level for being their dutiful submissive. It felt natural and she was compelled to pursue it further and find out what else she was capable of under the false veneer she'd projected to accommodate others. She parted her lips.

"Yes, sir. I understand," she answered in a small, meek, submissive voice.

"Good girl," they both chorused seductively.

"Everything doesn't start for another twenty minutes. It is your turn to establish your own rules, Dylan but I will assist in her punishment, if you require," Mark offered, trailing his fingertips along Drew's bare shoulder and sending tiny shivers down the length of her spine to erupt in a wave of wetness between her thighs.

Dylan grinned and began to direct her into the corner of the doorway away from the street. Luckily none of the guests was milling around this side entrance to the building and she prayed her spanking would not be seen or heard. But she should have known the twins were far too protective to have her bared and seen by anyone else. They had it all in hand.

Dylan pulled her against him in the corner and his brother positioned himself behind. Their bodies brushed Drew's and she was made aware of their hard cocks demanding to be inside her pushing against her bottom and vagina through the dress. She held her breath and waited.

"Lift her dress," Dylan instructed his brother.

Mark's hands around Drew's waist moved and skimmed over her hips taking time to appreciate the curves of her figure. She tried to watch as he bent down on his haunches and his hands traveled down her legs, pausing to hold her calves possessively, but Dylan cupped the side of her face and commanded her attention.

"Eyes front, darling. Don't disobey me again."

Mark's hands reached the bottom of her dress and for a moment he held her ankles tightly, making her think he had placed restraining cuffs around them. She forced herself to take a breath. Dylan was watching her the whole time, gazing into her eyes with loving stern command. Her body melted against him. Then she felt the cool evening breeze caress her bare calves. Mark was lifting her dress.

Nervously, she reached out her hands and gasped as she pushed them against Dylan's chest to hold on. He appeared to like her sudden anxious discomfort at being publicly exposed and the way she held onto him like a child by the sensuous curl of his lips.

Her dress rose higher between the two men and now it was skimming over her silk red panties to settle at her waist.

"Hold it while I take off her panties," Dylan instructed.

Mark grinned at his brother.

"I am looking forward to this."

Dylan let go of her face and lowered his body. She felt his hands over her buttocks and then one of them skimmed across the silk and lace V-shape of her panties at the front. A jolt of electricity shot through her body at his touch, making a small moan escape her tightly pursed lips. Then his fingers were tucking under the flimsy material at the sides and her panties were sliding and curving down her thighs.

The air brushed Drew's clit as it was exposed to the night air, making it tingle and ache with anticipation. Mark caressed his fingers over her buttock in a circular motion as the other hand held her dress up while Dylan pulled her thong panties down to her ankles and then lifted one high-heeled red-and-silver sandal up out of them with seductive care.

He turned his attention to the other. Drew made the mistake of moving and found Mark's hand winding around to the front of her body and her abdomen to hold her steady and in place. He stroked his hand over the gentle curve of her stomach as though to placate her with the stroke of his fingertips skimming the neatly shaven mound of hair that covered her vagina but refusing to enter the folds.

Dylan raised himself from the ground, holding her panties in one hand. But suddenly he stopped, his lips just inches from her pussy. His breath caressed her clit, making her tremble with need. She wanted to beg him to touch it, pinch it, and knead it to satisfaction, but out of respect to her master she remained quiet.

His hand slid over her thigh and she became aware of him studying her sex.

"She's wet, Mark. I want her like this all of the time so we can take her wherever and whenever we wish. One of my rules to add to the list."

She expected to feel the touch of his hand, but it was the gentle lick of his tongue she felt against the tiny wet jewel. Drew moaned. He lapped again. The aim of his wet caress was with precision. He touched only the clit and nowhere else.

A heavy ache to be penetrated fluttered into life. So far the twins had played with her, introduced her to their discipline and their rules, but they were yet to ride her together. She prayed it would be soon.

"Please, I want…I need to be penetrated. How much longer must I wait to have you both inside me?" she blurted out, forgetting her place.

Dylan moved his face away from her pussy and cupped it with his large hand. She gave a small yelp when he spanked it hard twice. He shook his head. Drew blushed, casting her eyes downward like a naughty girl.

"You have just earned yourself five extra strokes when I get that bottom of yours bared for discipline, little one," he said with a fatherly tone.

He spanked her vagina again and her bare bottom bucked backward against Mark. He was hard and his sheathed length nestled between the crease of her buttocks through his tuxedo trousers. Her ache grew and her sex flooded.

"Part of your submission training involves being patient to be taken. This is a joint brother rule. It is our right to choose when, where, and how. You simply obey and part your thighs or bottom when we order it and take your pleasure when we allow it. Do I make myself clear, little one?" Dylan explained, swatting her sex twice more.

"Yes, Daddy, yes," she answered breathlessly.

Dylan stood and towered over her again in his tuxedo, making her feel small and enticingly fragile in their protective hold.

She watched Mark deposit her panties in his pocket.

"Lower her dress. I need a room for what I have in mind," the spy told his brother.

Mark slid the dress down her legs and Drew tried to get used to the idea of being without any panties on underneath her dress after having them forcibly removed.

Dylan kissed her shoulder.

"Good girl. The hotel manager said we could use his office to make calls. We could take her there. We have fifteen minutes left," Mark informed them.

Dylan was cupping Drew's face again and brushing his lips against hers. She wanted to be kissed deeply, but he pulled back quickly when she reached for him. He wagged his finger at her.

"Naughty girl. Patience, little one. Soon. Before the night's end."

He looked at Mark over his shoulder.

"Let's get her there and get this bottom out in the open so she can be disciplined. We can't let this go," he said with determination, running his hand over her rump. "I thought we'd lost her to James—or worse, my father—tonight."

"I agree. Let's go."

Each brother took hold of one of Drew's arms and guided

her back indoors and down to the back end of the lobby to a corridor and an office.

16

Mark knocked on the door and opened it when he received no answer to check it was not occupied. He motioned for Dylan to lead Drew inside and then locked the door behind them.

Dylan wasted no time in taking her straight to the desk. He stood Drew in front of it and undid the zipper on the back of her dress. He quickly stripped her of the garment, leaving her standing in her strapless bra, her high-heeled sparkling sandals, and nothing else.

His eyes roamed over her body with lustful approval but then frowned when they rested on her bra.

"I need something to tie her hands with," he said to Mark as he reached behind her to undo the catch on her bra.

He lifted it away and tossed it onto one of the large padded chairs littering the white-and-gilt-edged office, greedily grabbing her breasts in his hands to knead and squeeze. Mark draped her dress over the chair. Then he searched the room and found to his surprise a roll of red satin draped over a woman's eighteenth-century costume on a mannequin. Raising his eyebrows, he brought it forward.

With a boyish grin, Dylan pulled Drew's wrists together. He

wound the satin material around them and tied it. Once more Drew was at their mercy and loving every moment, even though her heart skipped a beat every time she heard footsteps walking past the office and the chatter of guests.

Dylan raised her bound hands up into the air and cupped one of her breasts, making her cry when he cruelly gripped it.

"Now, little one, I am going to clear the desk and you are going to drape yourself across it face-down. But first…"

He lifted the panties out of his pocket.

"Open your mouth wide, baby girl," he instructed, bunching them into a ball. Pouting, Drew did as she was told and allowed him to insert the material in her mouth to use as a gag.

Drew hoped he would just spank her with his hand, but when he cleared the surface of the desk and led her to it, she could see he had other ideas.

As she lay over the desk with her tied hands stretched out in front of her dangling over the other side, her breasts squashing into the bound black leather and her wet sex pressing into the edge, she turned her head to see Dylan holding a long wooden ruler in his hand.

"This will do nicely," he said firmly.

Dylan widened her legs that were hanging above the desk.

There was nothing she could hide from him. Her heavily wet pussy hung open visible through her legs and her rump, still blushed a little pink from her early punishment, bared and vulnerable to the discipline Dylan was about to inflict upon it.

Dylan rested his hand on the small of her back and she became aware of him centering her again. The ruler rested across one of her buttocks. It felt cool, yet she knew it would soon burn her with its sting.

Dylan swept his hand around her throat in a gentle chokehold and guided her head to strain up and back from the desk. Mark bent down in front of her, his handsome face giving her a reassuring smile. He stroked her face to watch her facial expression as the ruler smacked down onto her bare bottom.

"Take a deep breath for me, little one," Dylan ordered. "And another," he repeated the action. "Now, one more, there's a good girl," he said softly.

Then the ruler left her bottom and she heard it whoosh through the air toward her flesh. Drew's body lifted and she tried to yelp with the hard, punishing strike of the ruler. But Dylan used his hold on her throat to guide her back down onto the desk. Mark watched her eyes widen and then close with each strike, enthralled as Dylan whipped her bare bottom with the ruler.

"We must keep you safe, kitten, and we will not tolerate your disobedience regarding our rules on your protection. Paul, James, and our father are dangerous men and this lesson must be learned well, darling. We were terrified for you."

Tears sprang into her eyes as the spy struck her bottom over and over again. Nevertheless, she could feel her sex flooding.

Drew was given twenty thwacks with the ruler and she knew fine well that Dylan was being lenient when he avoided the backs of her thighs, wanting her to be comfortable for the rest of the evening. When he brought her chastisement to an end, he rested his palm gently over her burning bottom, bowing to brush it with butterfly kisses, pressing the heat from it to his mouth.

"Well done, baby girl. You did well. One more of my rules and no doubt Mark's. Don't think I won't discipline you for bad behavior wherever we are. I want total obedience at all times, little girl, or you will be over my knees, a chair, a desk, or whatever else I can find to spank you over. Do you understand me?" he said in a dark velvet voice, kissing her bottom once more.

Mark stroked his fingers through the silky strands of her hair.

"Yes, Sir, I understand."

"Good." Dylan turned to Mark. "Did you bring them?"

"Yes. They are right here."

Mark stood up and took something from his pocket. It was a small box. Next he produced a small tube of lubricant. Drew stared at him, trying to work out what they were both talking about.

"I can't wait to put them inside her," Dylan said, helping Mark raise her from the desk.

"It's going to be interesting," Mark said with a wicked smile.

Dylan surprised her by bending to lift an arm up under her legs and scooped her up into his arms. He laid her on top of the desk face-up. Her legs dangled to the floor and he moved them upward and wide apart.

Dylan moved in front of Drew's thighs and caressed his finger through Drew's ripe damp sex, flexing the small bud back and forth under Mark's watchful gaze. She moaned gently, resting her bound hands on her stomach only to find herself corrected by Mark, who placed them above her head again and moved behind her so he could hold them there.

"You are nice and wet, Drew. Soaking wet in fact, and I will only need a little lubricant to insert these inside your vaginal channel," Dylan informed. "This is going to give you so much pleasure, little one, if you are obedient and do as you are told," he warned as though she were a child and capable of terrible naughtiness.

"What are they?" she asked breathlessly and nervously as she felt him pulse a finger up inside her channel to stretch and prepare her.

"Ben Wa balls."

He held them up to her. They were two medium-sized steel balls on a string.

"Every time you move they are going to arouse you and make you want to cum, kitten. But you have to hold your pleasure until one of us gives you permission to release it. This will be a good test for you as a submissive. Now widen your legs a little further."

Drew parted her thighs more and felt Dylan peel back the lips of her vagina. At first he closely examined her sex and then covered the balls in a small amount of lubricant just like he said he would. A moment later Drew felt him slide the balls inside until she was full to the brim.

It was a strange sensation, but when she shifted on the desk they rubbed at the walls of her vagina and sent a jolt of pleasure through her core. The act produced a helpless cry from her lips. Dylan grinned at his brother and pulled the string on the balls, moving them back and forth inside her. Drew panted, feeling controlled, her arousal building strongly. Then it stopped.

"Come on, we need to get going," Mark said, glancing at his

watch. "Are you ready for your small speech? I want you to do it first after I have made my own short one before the entertainment starts. Then there will be an auction and a ball. We can play more afterward."

Drew nodded, wondering how she would be able to keep sane delivering her speech and plea for information.

Dylan straightened and helped her down from the desk as she was forced to tighten her pelvic floor to keep the balls contained. He grinned and untied her hands.

"They are going to keep you nice and tight and very wet in there until we are ready to mount you. Mind you keep them in there, darling. We wouldn't want them falling out now, would we?" he said, amused.

Drew was allowed to dress minus her panties, correct her hair piled neatly on top of her head, and reapply her lipstick before they peered out of the door to check they could leave without being noticed.

She was led back to the lobby and into the hall at the center table in the front row of fifty dinner tables. Everyone was shouting hello to Mark and demanding their attention, but eventually they were seated with two of Mark's business associates and another disguised Interdefense agent.

Drew was relieved to sit down and not have to concentrate on holding the balls inside her. Mark left them to make his speech and then announced Drew, giving her full credit as the successful, award-winning investigative journalist she was. With confidence, she strode up onto the stage accompanied by her Dylan, her Interdefense protector and dual lover to deliver her plea and support for Mark's cause.

"I have also been the victim of domestic abuse. Many victims believe they are the cause and at fault. Years of violent abuse wears the victim down until they no longer see themselves a separate living entity and are a slave and more than often a punching bag for their partner to release their frustrations upon. It becomes their only clouded reason for existence. In essence they come to believe themselves subhuman and of no consequence only in relation to their partner and his—or sometimes her—needs. We need to support and counsel them to see their own worth and their right to a free, independent, joyful life free of violence in safety. With your help and support tonight, we can do that and provide a new life for victims."

Mark and Dylan looked at her with concern and sympathy for her words. Dylan stroked her arm as he stood next to her and the audience clapped. Dylan took his cue.

"As Drew said earlier, if anyone knows any information about the whereabouts of Eva Sumner, please call the number on the screen and your call will be taken in confidence. It is vital we find her as soon as possible."

Once more the audience clapped and the two left the stage.

Mark stood as they approached and kissed Drew. "You were wonderful. I had no idea that was how he made you feel. God, I wish I had been there for you!"

"You are now. I should have come to you," she said tearfully. "You were right."

He hugged her and pulled out her chair for her.

Just before the entertainment on the stage began, Drew received a new instruction from Dylan and Mark.

"Lift your dress under the tablecloth. We want to be able to touch you when we please," Dylan commanded on behalf of both of them. "Think of it as another rule," he whispered in her ear. "You must always be open and accessible for our touch."

"Yes, sirs," she said demurely, reaching to lift her dress underneath the tablecloth, thankful that it trailed the floor excitedly and wondering what her two lovers would do to her next.

17

Drew walked into the lounge late that evening wondering where the boys had got to after showering with her before going to bed. She put her hand to her mouth when she spied Dylan lying unconscious on the floor and Mark held at gunpoint. Her instinct was to rush toward Dylan to check him out, but the two men with Paul Dexter grabbed hold of her and held her still.

"I need to see him and make sure he is all right. Let Mark go!" she shouted, trying to protect them both.

"Drew, stay still and calm. He is just unconscious. He will be fine," Mark told her with heavy concern in his voice. "Please. I don't want you hurt."

Paul moved toward her struggling form.

"Do as you are told. There's a good girl," he said with an amused curl of his lips. "My, you are a feisty one. I am going to enjoy breaking you."

"Don't dare touch her or I will kill you," Mark demanded.

Paul just laughed at him and stretched out his hand to whip the towel away from Drew's body, leaving her naked. He dropped it to the floor and stared at her with admiration. But to Mark's relief, he did not touch her.

Drew whimpered, embarrassed, her cheeks flushing crimson. She looked at Mark with pleading eyes and his heart felt as though it had been stabbed. He moved toward her but was stopped by the end of the weapon being pushed into his forehead.

"Leave her alone, Paul."

"Bring the cage and make him silent," Paul demanded.

The man holding the gun at Mark's temple banged it against his forehead and knocked him out cold.

One of the men with Paul brought forward a cage. Paul took hold of Drew's arm and brought her to her knees on the ground in front of him. The man opened the cage and lifted her lowered, naked form to place her in the human-sized cage naked.

"Let me go," she screamed, struggling and unable to defend herself as the man confined her in the cage, closing the door quickly.

Paul bent down.

"You look beautiful confined."

Drew closed her fingers around the small wire bars and shook the cage, roaring with rage.

"Like a beautiful tigress. Don't worry—I will shave your claws and you will learn to please me in my bed. Cover the cage and carry her out. And if you are a good girl I will let you see your daughter again."

One of the stocky men grinned and covered the cage with a black cloth before raising the handle in the hole in the middle to carry it outside. Paul and his men followed and hurried out the back entrance of the hotel. Drew's cries for Dylan and Mark were muffled by the cloth as they carried the cage to a car and drove off into the night.

About the Author

Thought Catalog, it's a website.

www.thoughtcatalog.com

Social

facebook.com/thoughtcatalog
twitter.com/thoughtcatalog
tumblr.com/thoughtcatalog
instagram.com/thoughtcatalog

Corporate

www.thought.is